Dommie's nearness stirred sensations that had been dormant for all of my life before her. I knew those years were but a prelude, a preparation. When her fingers had touched mine that day, that long-ago day on the steps of her home, and her eyes smiled into mine, I found the future, and my fulfillment.

We helped each other undress and, naked, entered our bed. I turned to her and raised on an elbow. "I want to love you the way it feels good to me. I want to touch you with my lips." And I kissed her, a slow, soft kiss. "I want to touch you with my tongue." I outlined her lips with my tongue then I leaned and outlined a nipple. "I want to be close to you." I raised myself above her then lowered my body to hers. "I want to feel you soft and warm against me . . ."

SOUTH OF THE LINE

SOUTH OF THE LINE

by Catherine Ennis

The Naiad Press Inc.
1989

Printed in the United States of America
First Edition

Edited by Christi Cassidy
Cover design by Pat Tong and Bonnie Liss
    (Phoenix Graphics)
Typesetting by Sandi Stancil

Library of Congress Cataloging-in-Publication Data

Ennis, Catherine, 1937—
    South of the line : a novel / by Catherine Ennis.
        p. cm.
    ISBN 0-941483-29-0 : $8.95
    I. Title.
PS3555.N6S68 1989
813'.54--dc 19
                                                        88-31308
                                                        CIP

To Linda
for beating the bushes

About the Author

Catherine Ennis, a southerner by birth, still lives in the deep south, enjoying the best features of New Orleans and Houston and all the rich culture and history of that region. She lives with her lover of over fifteen years and assorted dogs, cats, fish and birds in a semi-rural area where such extended families are still possible. A little gardening, sculpturing and good eating are among her favorite pastimes. Author of *To The Lightning*, this is Catherine's second novel.

SOUTH OF THE LINE

CHAPTER I
Tuesday, December 17, 1861

Eight days before Christmas, my home, the only one I had ever known, burned to cinders in a blaze so fierce that the very bricks exploded. Neighbors say the flames were whipped by winds which carried sparks high enough to be seen from a mile distant.

Whether the fire that destroyed all but one blackened pillar was caused by accident or design I'll never know because my father, along with his manservant, was incinerated in the blaze.

Had I been home would I have suffered the same fate? I doubt it. I wish to believe that the disaster was an accident caused by too much drink or carelessness, that both conditions would have been prevented had I been there on that frozen night.

Too much drink, I knew, was a direct and continuing result of many business losses from which my father's finances could not seem to recover. The seriousness of the matter was brought home to me when I learned that I was next to penniless except for certain certificates which bore my name, the trunk of clothing I had carried with me for the Christmas visit to my aunt, my mother's jewelry, and the few good pieces of my own. Even the ground under the smoking ruins of my home did not belong to me, having been mortgaged to the hilt.

It is simply not in my nature to swoon at adversity; I am practical and independent. These two qualities probably contributed greatly to my single status but there was nothing I cared to do about that. Over the next sad days I took stock but found little encouragement in my situation.

In desperation, I planned to work for my living as a teacher. I was fluent in three languages and knowledgeable in astronomy, mathematics, geography, literature, grammar, composition, biology, and a smattering of other sciences which my father had said might prove useful some day.

In the weeks that followed my father's death I sent letters of application to many well-known institutions of learning. With so many men enlisting in the war to restore the Union, I felt that I had a good chance of finding employment. Not so.

For whatever reason — perhaps I lacked the proper qualifications or simply because of my sex — I did not receive one encouraging reply. I lowered my sights and inquired of smaller institutions, those teaching younger pupils. Again, there was no interest in what I had to offer.

I would have been greatly welcomed in some small town that supported a single teacher for the entire student body but my courage quailed at the thought of living from month to month with whatever family would speak for me. I am a private person and wished to remain so.

Though I loved my aunt dearly, I did not want to live with her and was too proud to accept her total financial assistance. She was a caring, generous person and her plan for me, as she explained delightedly, was to formally introduce me into her social milieu so that I might at last meet some man who would be willing to rescue me from my maiden state. Happiness, for Aunt Clarissa, was marriage and children and managing a home. Her three daughters felt likewise and they lived near enough that I would be subjected to constant pressure from the four of them. Thus, when she spoke the word "governess" to me, I told her, my spirits flagging, that I would take anything that gave me some vestige of independence.

"You have a distant cousin by marriage in Nashville who was widowed by yellow fever in fifty-three. She has a girl of ten, I believe, and a boy a year younger. I'll write to her," Aunt Clarissa offered.

The cousin wrote back, "Yes. Come in June. For safety the children have been taken to New Orleans so we'll have time to find out if we like each other

3

before moving to be with them at Christmas." Her answer pleased me for I had the same reservations. The stipend she mentioned was generous; the contract was made.

We read war news in *Harper's Weekly* and the New York *Tribune*. Distantly, we felt the seriousness of the conflict but last year's skirmishing had been far away. It was not until July and the Southern victory at Bull Run that the war had come close to our door. Even so, Uncle Harold stated that a stunted agricultural economy could not prevail against a balanced industrial one. "We have a logistical advantage," he pronounced. Whatever this meant, we instantly agreed in order to hush his daily and lengthening lectures on military strategy.

Thousands of young men had died since the bloodless bombardment of Fort Sumpter but their numbers were just that, figures from a newspaper column which moved us to pity. When my cousin Eva's husband enlisted as an officer in the Union army, the war first touched our lives in a personal way. At the end of February, however, the war became a direct concern for me: Nashville was occupied by the Union army.

After three weeks, hand-carried by messenger, a single line arrived from Mrs. LeCompte: "Faith, There is no change in plan. Dominique." I was reassured by her thoughtfulness.

Then, late in April, New Orleans also fell to the Union. Another letter from Dominique informed me that this would not cause a change in plan. She wrote that rail and river traffic was open and would probably remain so. She reminded me that Nashville had been occupied by the Federals since February and this had caused no undue hardship. Anyway, her two children were expecting her. She underlined the last words heavily which made me believe that my cousin was a woman true to her word.

It occured to me that Dominique and I must have opposite feelings, a completely different outlook, on this war which was increasingly soaking the earth with blood. Although my birth state of Illinois had taken little part in the political maneuvering which began this conflict, and had done hardly more in the year since, I felt loyalty to the Union and to its preservation.

The South's bristling anger over the election of Mr. Abraham Lincoln to the office of president had seemed overdone to me. They were so loud in arguing their right to protect their domestic institutions that they didn't hear our new president declare in his inaugural address that he would not interfere with slavery in the states where it existed. How could it have been put plainer?

Now, my cousin, a slave-owning Southerner, was already garrisoned. The cities under seige were her cities; the capturing army was mine. Would this cause us not to be friends? My feeling for her was almost set: I liked her, sight unseen. I was looking forward to Nashville and New Orleans, and wanted to begin my new life without burdens from the old.

The first week in June, on a Monday morning, I bid farewell to my only close relatives and to the life that had been mine up to that moment. Turning from Aunt Clarissa's tearful embrace, I stepped aboard the train, settled myself on a hard wooden seat, and waited for the wheels to turn.

CHAPTER II
June, 1862

At last in Nashville, weary beyond description, I descended from the train. The station was hot and crowded with Union soldiers. The entire place was an ant bed of steaming blue uniforms.

I was hungry, tired, dirty, gritty, and my head still throbbed from breathing the engine fumes that had been forced into my open window by the movement of the train. I wanted to go home, to my comfortable rooms that were cool and smelled of sun-dried linens and years of polished wax, but which were now only blackened ashes. I did not want to be here. I leaned against one of the posts that supported the shed-like roof of the station, closed my eyes and tried to remember why I had come in the first place.

Someone touched my arm. I jerked my eyes open and looked . . . up . . . and up . . . and up. A giant colored man was smiling down at me, his huge hand laid delicately on my wrist. He bent until he was more or less on my level and touched his chest with his finger. Then he pointed to me with the same finger and nodded, pointing again to himself. I swallowed hard, an audible gulp, then realized harm was not his intent nor was he begging. My transportation had arrived.

I waited with as much patience as I could muster for the train attendants to locate my trunk; finally it was lifted casually to one huge shoulder. Amid confusion such as I had never seen, I followed it and the shoulder to a waiting carriage. With as much ease as if the trunk had been empty, my coachman put it on the rack and then helped me as I climbed the step to my seat. So far he had not spoken.

"You were sent by my cousin, Mrs. LeCompte?" I said to his back.

No answer. But he turned and smiled at me and nodded.

Well, at least he could hear.

With a sigh, I leaned back against the leather cushions, not at all enjoying the heat that settled over me like a blanket, causing perspiration to run from under my hat, drip from my chin and soak my collar. My delicate lace handkerchief was of no help. What I needed was a sponge.

As we moved away from the station I saw that the carriage was beautifully appointed and sparkling. The man's black suit was immaculate, fitting him as if it had been tailored. Of course, it would almost have to be, no hand-me-down would stretch across those massive shoulders.

I could not see but I could hear the horse and I liked the pattern made by the hooves; this animal was healthy, spirited and wanted to run. My coachman's touch was light, just enough to hold the animal without roughness. All of this was to my liking and my spirits lifted considerably.

We passed from the sweltering, crowded town and the melange of idle soldiers to a well-kept road that passed between heavy trees that often met overhead. It was cooler in the shade and, on a whim, I removed my hat to let some of the breeze fan my temple.

After some distance, my carriage turned off the road, pulling through two ornate iron gates and I saw the place that was to be my home until I moved to New Orleans. If I met my cousin's standards, that is. The mansion was lovely, with clean white lines and tall windows that reflected light like diamonds in a stone setting. As we drew near the glass entrance doors, one of them opened and two women descended the stone steps that fronted the lower floor. One woman, I could see, was colored. The other was probably Mrs. LeCompte. How nice of her, I thought, to greet me personally.

It was not she, however. The one with the lightest coloring spoke to my driver, calling him Henry. I stepped down from the carriage, with Henry's hand to assist, and started up the steps. Then, at the sound of horses approaching, Henry and the two women

8

turned towards the gates, as did I. What a sight met my eyes!

There were two horses galloping straight across the grassy circle, headed directly for the carriage. I knew there was to be a collision. Even the best of riders would find it difficult to stop or swerve that crashing advance short of leaping directly over the carriage and onto the steps. I moved off the steps and to the side, not noticing that the other three people about to be trampled had not moved except to get a better view.

The horses approached so rapidly that I could only glimpse the two riders, both young men — one colored, one white. Hooves pounding and clods of dirt flying, the horses braked and reared, stopping within an inch of the carriage, the riders howling with laughter.

The white boy threw one leg across the saddle and sat sideways, both he and the horse breathing hard. He turned to the other rider who was heading back towards the gates, and yelled, "Beat you again! You might as well give up, Hank!"

Hank hollered over his shoulder, "There'll be a next time!"

Now I turned my attention to the young man who had guided his horse in front of me. I looked up into bright green eyes and an impish grin . . . a woman's face. This was no boy! She wore men's clothing, filthy breeches, a rough white shirt open at the throat, rolled up at the sleeves, and mud-caked, scuffed boots. A long black pigtail escaped from under her faded, floppy hat. I gaped and the woman's grin widened, showing even, white teeth in a dazzling smile.

"Hello!" she said, leaning to offer her hand, "I'm Dominique. We've all wondered what you'd look like!" Her smile seemed to say that she was not disappointed in what she saw. I reached to touch her fingers, in the token kind of handshake that women use, but she took my entire hand in hers and held it . . . her hand was sweaty and not too clean. We looked at each other over our clasped fingers and . . . I gave up all thoughts of escape.

Dominique sat up and I let go of her hand . . . or she released mine. "Henry, do you know where to go with those?" She indicated my trunk and valises with a movement of her head.

Henry nodded and lifted the trunk; I think he could have managed the carriage, too. The darker of the two women took the bags. I started to follow and heard, "If you're not too tired, Faith, would you eat with me tonight? I'd love company."

I turned and looked at her again from higher up the steps. A leather belt bound her slender waist and the tight breeches outlined her lower form. She was leaning towards me and the open shirt could not conceal her bosom, unbound, the contour of each breast straining the rough fabric. I was having trouble with my breathing but I managed to say, "Certainly, I'd love to."

* * * * *

The dining room was huge, the table could have seated thirty, but we were only two. There was soft candlelight and cool wine, delicious food, heavy silverware, the perfection of Limoges porcelain and

10

hand-painted veilleuses, flawless service from the maids and . . . Dominique.

She, now in a plain house gown fastened demurely at the neck, was seated at the head of the table and I on her right, close enough to touch hands again. That thought sneaked into my head as I watched her slender fingers stroke the stem of her goblet. It was not a nervous movement. More that she enjoyed feeling the delicate crystal curves.

We did not talk much while eating. Her appetite matched mine and we both took second servings. Then, when the plates were cleared, we had coffee. She sat, relaxed, casually watching as I sipped. I was unaccountably nervous and spoke to break the silence, "Antoinette and Elsas are well?"

"Yes," she nodded, "They write almost every day and the sisters send a bundle of letters when someone comes this way. It seems Elsas misses his pony most of all." She paused, then asked, "Do you ride?"

I shrugged and smiled, indicating yes.

"We have stables behind the house. You may ride whenever you choose." The light from the candles showed little gold flecks in the green of her eyes. They seemed to catch and reflect the soft glow. I liked watching her mouth as she spoke. I wished she'd say more.

"Is there anything you'd like to do while we wait for October? We have a library and a garden, even a music room if you play."

"Yes, I play the harpsichord and piano . . . and I read." Dumb! Of course I'd have to read.

Her smile encouraged me so I said, "But, isn't there some useful activity . . . I'd not like to be idle."

11

I thought she was reaching for my hand but she picked up the almost empty goblet and drained it. "I'm afraid most activities are spoken for already. You could ride." She shrugged. "And amuse yourself somehow."

I felt like a child being told to go play. In fairness, at twenty-three I probably seemed like a child to her; she was at least thirty. I finished my coffee and heard, "You're tired from the long ride, I know. You probably want to rest?"

No, I wanted to sit here with her but I nodded.

She reached for my hand. Her fingers touched mine and I heard, "Goodnight, Faith. Sleep well." And she was gone. I had only the memory of a brief contact, her fingers brushing lightly for an instant.

Mine was a corner room on the second floor and had windows on two sides. The right side, as one entered the door, faced the front of the house. Huge moveable shutters hung outside each window and I could have walked upright through the openings to the narrow balcony that fronted the house.

It was a lovely room with a large fireplace, and the floor was covered with a deep rug. The windows were framed by heavy drapes which were held aside by matching ties. Altogether, I could be very comfortable here.

I readied myself for bed then crawled into the depths of a feather mattress and fell asleep instantly. Only once during the night did I wake. I heard horses pounding down the drive, heading away from the house.

* * * * *

12

The pattern of each day was uneventful. I slept, ate, walked in the garden, looked without interest at the library shelves, played the out-of-tune piano, tried to write, spoke to no one, became very bored. The only bright spot was Dominique when she was in residence. I must call it that because she seemed to be away from the house much of the time. I would hear her leaving at breakneck speed, the horses pounding down the drive and out the gate at dusk. On those nights I would eat alone. If she ate at all, it was not in the dining room with me.

A few times at dawn I heard the horses returning, walking slowly, to stop under my window. In a few minutes I would hear Dominique's bedroom door close softly. She would sleep until the early afternoon, then I would see her at the library desk, her dark head bent in concentration over one of the many letters she wrote to her children in spite of the disruption in the federal mail service. Hearing me, she would look up and her smile would invite me into the room. I would sit quietly, pretending to read, listening to the scratch of her pen, watching her over my book. Often, just to be near her, I would sit in the library waiting for her to come downstairs so that she could smile at me, so that we could talk.

The first time we walked in the garden she took my arm, her fingers touching possessively as she guided me along the paths. This closeness, this familarity, was foreign to me and I walked stiffly, almost rigid with embarrassment but keeping step so as not to break the contact. Soon it became her habit to take my hand as we strolled and I found myself eagerly lacing fingers with her. I looked forward to those quiet moments, drawing them out as long as I could.

One afternoon, Dominique guided me from the path to a shaded spot beneath an oak. "Sit where I can look at you," she said, setting her back against the tree. So I sat on the ground before her and stared at my hands, unable to look at her, my face flaming under her scrutiny. Without a word, she moved to her knees and leaned, catching the ends of the ribbon that bound my hair, pulling away the knot so that my hair fell loose around my shoulders. I was too astonished to speak. "Lovely," she said. "Lovely." Then she rose, clasped my hand to help me to my feet and, her fingers still gripping tightly, led me back to the walkway.

I stayed awake for hours that night, staring at the ceiling, thinking of my life, wondering if anyone had ever died of loneliness.

I was, however, waited on hand and foot. Malissa, the woman of lighter color who had met me that first day, seemed to be in charge of the household. I heard her at times but saw her infrequently. I seldom saw anyone as I wandered aimlessly through the downstairs rooms.

Remembering Dominique's offer of a horse, I found my way to the stable and my life changed dramatically thereafter.

I met Uncle Ham, the colored man in charge of the stables. When I saw the pristine condition of the stalls, the shining tack room, the fresh feed and sweet-smelling hay, I knew that in him I had found someone I could respect. I told him so.

At home I had learned to ride astride, impossible to do in a dress, so Uncle Ham located worn boots and threadbare pants and I made a loose-fitting shirt from one of my old nightgowns. I now spent many early hours at the stables, helping with the horses and the two frisky ponies who no longer had children giving them exercise. I talked with Uncle Ham, telling him about myself because I was grieving and homesick and he was kind enough to listen.

Most mornings several of the horses would appear hard-ridden and exhausted and I knew it was because Dominique had taken a night ride with her friends. Or whatever it was that she did. Uncle Ham did not say and I did not pry.

Dominique's prize was a stallion called Spirit. He was coal black and Uncle Ham curried him until he glistened. Someone had worked with him at one time but he had not been ridden much and needed further training. For this, Uncle Ham was too old. I was not.

I worked with Spirit . . . it became such a pleasure to spend time with him. He learned to come to me when I snapped my fingers, to move at just the slightest touch to the reins, like Dominique's hand on mine that first night. I rode for hours, sometimes galloping at his great speed, often just meandering along the Cumberland's high bluffs, trying to get my thoughts in order.

I seemed unable to sort through my grief or the feeling of confusion that filled me. I would picture my father's dear face, wishing I could have reached through flames to rescue that gentle man. Then my heart would race, remembering Dominique's slow smile, the soft pressure of her fingers.

I found it harder and harder to dismiss her from my thoughts. Her face would appear to me at the oddest times, superimposed on whatever page I was reading or floating with the clouds as I daydreamed. Very distressing!

Word of the fighting came from Dominique's friends in Nashville and she gave me information as it was given her. We knew, for example, of General Lee's strike against McClellan at Mechanicsville, Virginia the day after it took place. Later, we were anguished to learn that almost thirty thousand men had been killed or wounded in those seven days' battles that gained nothing for either side. Dominique would tell me what she knew, but would not introduce debate, so our differences, if any, were not a subject for discussion.

Our conversations were often innocuous, like strangers with nothing in common but the need for politeness. Dominique, her smile empty and her mind clearly not on me, would say, "How was your day, Faith?" And I, taking her cue, would answer simply, "Fine, Dominique." "Is there anything you need, Faith?". . . "No, thank you, Dominique, I have what I need."

But I really didn't. Even Spirit couldn't seem to fill a void that had opened before me.

CHAPTER III
July, 1862

We were at lunch together.

"I'm having a few guests for dinner on Monday, Faith. I'd be pleased if you'd join us." She smiled at me, friendly as ever but distant. "It will be rather formal. Do you have something to wear?"

Trying to look equally friendly but just as distant, I nodded. "Yes, I have a thing or two; everything wasn't burned. I'll be happy to meet your friends."

Her smile told me that she was pleased. I wondered if I was to be presented as the children's governess or as the impoverished Northern cousin or, perhaps, the pitiful young woman who had been graciously taken in after losing both father and home.

These thoughts were unkind but I was not feeling charitable. Dominique had not been in the house for two days, off on one of her trips, and I felt cross, irritable. I know it was foolish of me but I did not want her going wherever it was she went; I wanted her here. I had no right to feel this way but I am able to control my feelings only after I've had them . . . not before. Many times each day I made an effort to clear my thoughts of Dominique . . . but in order to do that, I had first to bring her to mind. I was unhappy without knowing the reason.

"Would you like to ride with me this afternoon?"

I jumped at the chance. "Yes, thank you, I would."

Dominique had changed into pants and shirt, the boots dirtier than ever, and she had carelessly plaited her long hair so that it hung down her back. She was carrying the floppy hat, slapping it against her leg as we walked to the stables and causing all manner of dust to fly.

Uncle Ham greeted us courteously and asked which horse Miss Dominique wanted today . . . She told him and then they both turned to look at me . . . and what was I to say? I became flustered and felt my face turning red; I had not told her of the time I spent with Uncle Ham or about Spirit and now I regretted the lapse.

Dominique began to laugh aloud. "Uncle Ham, saddle Spirit for my cousin while I help her change."

18

I was mortified!

Dominique took my elbow and led me to the tack room, shutting the door firmly once we were inside. The room was small and when I turned to face her we were only inches apart. "You knew?" I asked.

"Of course I knew, dear, it's my business to know what goes on around this place. I'm glad you found some way to entertain yourself. Spirit is probably pleased, too. Now, dress and let's see what you've done with my horse."

Leaning against the door, she made no move to leave. I had to reach around her to lift my pants and shirt from their nail, then struggle to lift my dress over my head without touching her. Managing that was not too difficult . . . but now I stood in my tight undergarments which needed to be removed in order to sit astride. I could not meet her eyes and I refused to turn my back. We were both women, after all.

She smiled at my obvious discomfort and said softly, "Would you like for me to leave, little girl?"

Embarrassed and furious because of it, I shook my head. My eyes still avoiding hers, I removed my chemise then slipped the shirt over my arms, pulling it closed and fastening each tiny loop with deliberation. With my face now burning hot, I stepped out of my pantalets and, conscious of my nakedness from the waist down, pulled on first the right and then the left trouser leg, yanking to settle the rough fabric over my hips as quickly as I could. My fingers began fumbling helplessly with the front buttons. I tried to make it seem that I did this sort of thing every day but my hands wouldn't work and my throat was so dry I couldn't swallow. I could actually

19

feel her eyes. And where was my belt? Without it the pants would slide down to my knees.

"You're a lovely young woman." I heard her voice, soft, hushed. "Here, little girl, you'll need this."

I almost yanked the belt from her outstretched hand. Missing most of the loops, somehow I got it around my waist and buckled in the front. Then I snatched my boots from the floor and pushed past her to open the door. I had to get away from so much closeness. I sat on the bench against the outside wall and grappled with a boot. Dominique watched for a moment then knelt and took the boot from my hand. "This way," she said quietly and slipped the boot on my foot. I watched her take the other boot, felt her lift my foot and slip the boot on easily. "Now stand to settle them."

I wanted to tell her that I knew how to put on boots. I looked at her, my mouth opened and I think I was going to speak but Dominique's eyes stopped me. Almost level with mine, they were greener and deeper than I had ever seen them and they held me captive. She was not smiling now. Her lips were slightly parted and I saw her draw in a deep breath, heard her exhale slowly. We were standing like that, close but not quite touching, not speaking as Uncle Ham appeared leading the two horses.

The rest of the afternoon passed in a haze, at least for me. Dominique and I rode to the river, then past vast green fields of cotton, into the adjacent wooded areas which she also owned, gave our horses water at a small, clear stream, then made our way back toward the stable. We hardly spoke even though we rode side by side. I could feel that she was turned, watching me, but I could not meet her eyes; I could hardly keep my seat. I seemed to be bouncing helplessly in the saddle and as breathless as if I had been carrying Spirit instead of the other way around.

I am ill, I reasoned unhappily. The sun has addled my brain. Soon, I told myself, my bones will rattle with fever and I'll fall off this horse. Then, in a flash, as though lightning had struck, I knew that the cause of my distress came not from overhead but was riding the horse next to me. I became calm, all was clear. Well, not all.

I smiled at Dominique. Dominique smiled back, her face half-shaded by the hat. I rode ahead for a length or two then heard, "Faith."

I turned.

"I'm glad you came, my dear. Very glad."

"Yes," I said, "yes."

At the stable we parted, me to change back into my dress and she to ride to the house . . . late for something or other. I did not see her again until the night of the dinner.

* * * * *

One of the house servants, a woman whom I had not seen before, asked if I needed help in dressing my hair for the dinner. I was delighted at the offer of such sophisticated assistance but I hesitated, uneasy, because I had never had close personal service from a slave. After a moment, knowing the mess I would probably make of the intricate coiffure fashion dictated, I accepted.

I wore the gown that I had planned to wear Christmas Eve at Aunt Clarissa's party. It was cut low with shoulders bare, bosom uplifted and scandalously exposed, uncomfortably tight at the waist then flowing in soft folds to the floor. The deep blue color matched my eyes, my father had said, and the delicate gold lace brought out the gold tones in my auburn hair. I knew I would be more than a match for any of the other ladies present, especially if I wore my mother's necklace or the tiara which had been her favorite piece. This thought was curiously pleasing to me. I, who had never sought fashion or competition in the garments I wore.

I decided to wear the tiara. Dominique's newly orphaned relative, her children's governess, her diamond-encrusted cousin — I could be all or any one of the three. I did not feel dread at facing Dominique's friends. Her invitation had been casual; the evening had not been arranged in order to parade me as an eligible body. Aunt Clarissa could not have passed up this opportunity. "Faith, you turn up your nose before you get to know your suitors. You'll never get married if you don't give them an honest chance!" So be it.

I heard Malissa at Dominique's door, telling her that the guests were arriving so I put down my book, smoothed my gown and walked out into the hall. Dominique opened the door to her room at the same time.

When last I saw her she had been a tomboy — filthy boots, smelling of horse, her hair in disarray. Now, standing in her doorway, gowned, feminine, she was truly beautiful. Her dress was modestly low-cut, of some dark silken shade as befits a widow, but her hair was an ebony crown, with two soft swirls falling to her bosom, outlining the smooth, slender column of

22

her neck. The jewelry at her breast sparkled like bright stars in a clear, night sky. Slowly she released the knob and turned to face me.

We stood, unmoving, as Malissa descended the stairs. Dominique, too, was staring. I cannot say what thought possessed me but, with a longing like I'd never before felt, I held out my hand to her and she reached to take it in her own. We moved closer, our gloved hands clinging, and with her free hand she touched my cheek in a soft caress. I was aware of my heart pounding, of her smile and her green eyes. Slowly she drew me to her and our lips touched. I closed my eyes and gave myself to the kiss. After an eternity that lasted but a moment, she moved her mouth from mine. "Come now," she said quietly. "Our guests are waiting."

Except for those moments when I had Dominique's attention, the rest of the evening remains blurred in my memory.

Later, as I dressed for bed, I heard Hank speaking below my side window, saw him holding four horses. Then Dominique's slim figure, now in masculine attire, appeared. She mounted one horse, took the reins of a spare and, instantly at a full gallop, disappeared into the darkness behind the house.

CHAPTER IV
July, 1862

I could not remember such acute boredom. The library was filled with books, none of which I wished to read. The subjects may have been of some interest to me but the print was too small and the ideas so outdated that they read like fairy tales.

What to do! What to do!

I walked aimlessly through the garden, deliberately not thinking about Dominique who, I found, filled my thoughts more and more as the days passed.

It was mid-afternoon, too early for bed but too late to visit the stables. A ride would have been exhilarating but Uncle Ham would be busy and would not have time for me. I toyed with the idea of visiting, not riding, just a simple visit so, that there would be someone to answer when I talked and someone to talk to me.

I sighed, for the thousandth time, and headed for the gazebo, sure of shade and a place to sit. My dress was much too hot for the southern sun, perhaps I could loosen it a bit in the privacy of the little open octagonal room.

The shade was kinder than the sun but the afternoon breezes had not yet materialized and the stillness was heavy. I loosened a few buttons so that my neck and throat could cool; then, finding that pleasant, opened a few more buttons to expose what I could of my sweltering flesh. Why not? There was no one to see that I was wearing naught but the dress. The bench was hard but the wooden lounge, when I moved it to the shadiest area, was more comfortable than it looked. I lay with one arm supporting my head and allowed my mind to drift.

A drifting mind is fertile ground for imagination and my thoughts instantly turned to Dominique, dwelling on her startling green eyes, the sheen of her black hair, the softness of her lips, the taste of her mouth on mine. She was, I thought, as vibrant and alive as Spirit, both of them independent and elegant.

It crossed my mind that one did not compare women and horses but, with my eyes now closed, I pictured Spirit flying with me across the pasture, felt the wind loosening and blowing my hair and his powerful animal muscles moving between my legs. I thrilled at this image but there was another crowding for my attention; this one was of smooth white shoulders and a full, soft bosom, partially exposed by a low-cut gown.

Why did my thoughts constantly turn to Dominique? Even now, I felt my heart quicken when I remembered her hand in mine and the intensity of expression as she touched my cheek with her fingertips . . . then that breathless moment as we stared at each other, moving closer, our lips finally touching.

Heat suffused my face and neck as I recalled that moment. Admittedly, I lacked worldly wisdom but I was not so naive that I did not recognize the physical stirring within me as her mouth touched mine. Perhaps Southern ladies kissed this way routinely but I doubted it.

Thanks to the obligatory three years in a school for young ladies, I had learned the required social skills. From fellow students, however, I heard details of the intimacies that took place between the human male and female. I believed those whispered confidences to be correct since they reflected, in a more refined way, what I knew of the act of procreation between animals. My father had not been actively engaged in the day-to-day care of our stock but he supervised a program of selective breeding and I, unbeknownst to my father, had avidly watched the process. So, even though I lacked firsthand experience, I was more knowledgeable than most single ladies of my station.

Too, I was aware that there were variations in the patterns of activity that took place in the bedroom. It was explained to me that women could also perform the act of love together and that this was not only pleasurable but also preferred by some ladies. My participation in such an act had been solicited but I had declined out of shyness and fear. Thinking now about my feelings for Dominique, I wished I had accepted that bold offer. At least it would have given me some base from which to examine this longing of mine to have her kiss me again.

The sun, somewhat lower now, was losing its intensity and the light afternoon breeze was stirring. With no effort at all, still thinking of Dominique, I drifted into slumber.

* * * * *

I was awakened by a light touch on my arm. Startled, I opened my eyes.

"You sleep soundly, little girl."

Green eyes held mine. Dominique was sitting on the low stool next to my lounge, elbows propped on the wooden arm, chin resting on cupped hands, her face only inches from mine.

Confused, my mind still alive with a dream in which Dominique was even closer than at this moment, I found no words to say.

She smiled, her gaze deliberately dropping to my breasts which were almost totally exposed. Hastily I pulled the edges of my gown together and, with as much dignity as I could manage, swung my legs to the floor and sat up.

"How long have you been watching me?" I demanded, frightened by her closeness.

"Long enough." She was still smiling, enjoying my discomfort.

That enigmatic answer confused me even more. Long enough for what, I almost asked, but realized just in time that I wasn't ready for her reply, whatever it may have been. We stared at each other until, embarrassed by my own thoughts and the pounding of my heart, I looked down at my lap.

After a moment Dominique stood. "Come," she said almost brusquely. "I'm eating early and I'd like you with me at the table." She was now mistress of the manor, her green eyes fathoms deep as she turned and swept out of the gazebo without a backward glance.

Anger threatened to choke me but I rose and followed those slim shoulders, buttoning my gown as I went.

* * * * *

We ate in the small dining room, facing each other over glistening oak. Dominique was obviously distracted, her hand reaching often for the wine, taking deep draughts as if consumed by thirst. She ate only a mouthful of food before pushing her plate aside. This was such a change from her usual hearty appetite that I was intrigued. It was not my place to ask questions so I ate as slowly and calmly as I could, curious but still angered at her imperious manner.

Dominique, her fingers lightly touching the crystal stem of her glass, stared at something over my head. I tried not to meet her eyes when her gaze was lowered to my face but she said my name, so softly that I almost didn't hear.

"Faith." The word was almost a caress.

28

I raised my goblet, slowly sipping the cool liquid. I lowered my glass then touched the napkin lightly to my lips before replying.

"Dominique." I tried to look languid and bored.

My acting was more convincing than I intended it to be.

We were still looking at each other as she drained her glass, shoved back her chair, slammed the glass on the table and stomped out of the room.

I was trembling as I finished my meal, trying to act as if nothing had taken place and, in truth, I did not know what it was that had taken place.

I went directly to my room, pulled my favorite volume of poems from the tiny shelf then sat and stared blindly at the printed page, my mind racing. Had I gone too far? I was, after all, hardly more than a servant in this house, dependent upon Dominique's generosity. My pride, my personal idiosyncrasies, were of no importance in this household. I vowed to hold my temper in the future, to curb my curiosity. I was at the point of vowing to stop thinking about Dominique when I heard the clatter of hooves in the drive below my balcony.

Rushing to the window, I was in time to see three riders racing towards the gate. One of the riders, of course, was Dominique. Even from the back I could see that she was wearing breeches and a man's shirt. Her black braid had again escaped from under her floppy hat and now trailed behind her. I stood watching until the riders were lost from sight.

I read until the light faded then rang for hot water, bathed, dressed in my night clothes and returned to the sofa. Not sleepy and wondering where Dominique had gone, I idly turned pages in the dim light from my candles, then fell asleep, the book still in my hand.

* * * * *

It was the creaking of the door and the snap of the lock that awakened me. I was not alarmed but opened my eyes slowly, somewhat surprised to find that I was still on the tiny sofa. Then, as my sight cleared, I saw a figure standing over me, a man's silhouette against the window.

I started to cry out but a hand covered my mouth.

Several things happened in the next instant. First, I smelled horse; next, a sweet scent that could only belong to Dominique, and then my arms, moving of their own accord, reached to embrace the figure that leaned over me.

A lover's kisses are surely made in heaven. I have never tasted anything sweeter than the lips that were then pressed to mine. Sweet kisses, yes, but it was I and the desire that a dream had kindled that turned them into the passionate, wanton caresses we shared that night. It was I who pulled Dominique's slim form to the couch, inviting her to press, nay, to thrust her weight against me as I opened my mouth beneath hers. She lay on me, her tongue at first tentative as she tried to match its movement to the surging of my hips. Then the fire caught her and we were joined, as one, our mouths wet, warm, moving together. I felt a rush of heat where her body pressed, a tickle of wetness, and a desire that would take more than kisses to assuage.

Dominique sat up, finally, and removed her boots but it was I who fumbled open the buttons of her shirt, releasing her breasts so that I could touch them. I sat up and turned her in my lap so that I could have her mouth, could fondle her breasts at the same time. I wanted to slide my hand under the waist of her trousers, move down until I touched her soft private parts but my dream was not yet that bold so I held back, content with her mouth, her breasts, her body warm in my arms. We kissed until I was quite drunk with rapture, my heart pounding like a runaway herd.

The tiny couch became too small for our embraces and we moved to the huge bed that enclosed us in its softness. My gown was soon raised waist high, then remained bunched around my neck until impatient hands swept it to the floor and I lay, naked, in Dominique's arms. She leaned to my breast and enclosed a nipple within her warm mouth, sucking like a newborn. I felt her hand moving down my body but I caught her . . . not because I didn't want the feel of her but because I wanted her unclothed, too. "Take those off," I whispered and, when she did as I asked, I lay back and pulled her down to me, feeling her nakedness for the first time.

She sucked at my breasts, causing me to lose breath time and again. Boldly she touched between my legs, making my heart stop. I was wet there; I felt her fingers moving in the moisture that seemed to pour from me. Her fingers moved, and moved, and moved! Then, without conscious thought to prompt me, I pushed her from my breast and guided her down my body until my arms could reach no farther. She stopped, her head poised above my open legs. For a moment I saw her white face, then, with a deep sigh, she leaned into me and I felt her black hair

CHAPTER V
July, 1862

"Wake up."

Did I dream that whispered sound? I thought I felt a soft touch on my shoulder.

"Wake up."

I smelled the fragrance of sassafras tea. There was a reason for not opening my eyes but I couldn't remember what it was. Wait, there was another odor underlying that of the tea. My nose almost buried in the goose down pillow, I drew in a deep breath and the scent of Dominique's hair came to me. That, and on my hand and lips, the velvety odor of . . . of her body.

My eyes flew open. In absolute horror I stared at the cup of steaming tea held inches from my face. I moved my gaze upward, following the fingers that held the cup, up a slender arm to smooth, bare shoulders. It was she, Dominique, breasts uncovered . . . nay, not just uncovered . . . there was nothing around her shoulders to act as a covering. Only that long hair, loose, clinging to her like a silken cloud.

"Are you going to stare at me all morning? Move over and take your tea, I'm getting tired standing here." There was brusqueness in her tone — that and something else. Laughter? Surely not!

I rolled away from her, onto my back. Then I sat up, pulling the cover firmly under my chin.

"Take your tea, love."

Obediently I reached for the saucer, moving as I did, towards the opposite side of the bed so that our bodies would not touch as she lifted the covers and climbed in beside me. Memory was flooding back, an icy tidal wave of memory that froze me to the spot.

"Faith?" Her hand touched my thigh . . . my naked thigh . . . and stayed. I could feel my flesh burning under her fingers. "Is something wrong?"

I couldn't answer. My hands began shaking so hard that the cup clattered, dancing around on the saucer. I was helpless to stop it.

"Damn!" Dominique reached out from the cover, took the tea from me and put it on the tiny night table next to the bed. "Damn!" she said again, turning back to me.

I had closed my eyes so that I wouldn't have to look at her but she knelt by my side and cupped my face in her hands. "Faith, love, look at me!"

That was the second time she had called me "love." I took heart and opened my eyes to see her face very close to mine . . . very, very close. Our lips touched and I closed my eyes again. That exquisite softness! I felt her breath on my face, her tongue searching mine. All of last night came back to me then and my fear dropped away like leaves in autumn.

I reached for her, arms tightening around her slender waist, my heart exulting as I heard her sharp intake of breath. I kissed her, moving so that our naked breasts touched, felt her tremble as I pressed into her. Ah, yes, I knew what to do next. I had the experience of a whole night to guide me.

I slid from under the covering, pulling her down with me, turning my body to cover her warm nakedness. I moved from the sweetness of her mouth to taste each breast, my tongue making circles as my hand searched the moisture between her legs. I covered my fingers with wetness and began stroking the soft place that provided so much pleasure. Did she like for me to bite her nipple as I moved my hand? I experimented and found memory was correct.

How I gloried in touching her, touching all of her, touching lightly, gently, feeling her move under my hands, opening herself so that I might taste the juices that flowed so freely; then, her beautiful body suddenly stilled, rigid with the pleasure that I had given.

She wanted to make love to me, after, but I held her from it. "No." I whispered, "No, I want to love

35

you again." And I did, until she lay limp in my arms. Damp hair on her smooth forehead, eyes luminous as she looked up at me — "I love you," she breathed. "Oh, I love you."

"I love you, too." From the deepest part of me I said those words. "I love you with all my heart."

Her arms around my neck, a tiny frown. "Then why were you afraid?"

"Earlier, you mean? When you brought the tea?"

"Yes."

Her face was serious so I thought a moment before I answered. "I was remembering what we had done in the night, how we had . . . touched . . . and I was ashamed; afraid and ashamed."

"Ashamed? How could you be ashamed?" She was incredulous. "I feel no shame in what we do!"

Propped on my elbow, pressed against her silken warmth, I found it hard to concentrate and it was important to tell her my honest feelings. "No," I started slowly, "I don't either, but there are those that would." I moved to rest on my back and waited as she pillowed her head on my shoulder, her arm across my waist.

"I think that I've wanted to . . . to love you from the day we met. You looked down at me, remember, and then you held out your hand and I felt something when our fingers touched. Maybe I fell in love with you then." These words were difficult, for I had never spoken of my deepest feelings to anyone. "All these weeks I've thought about you but I didn't know what to do about the way I felt. I had no idea you felt the same. Then we kissed, remember? And in the gazebo, when you looked at me, your expression was so strange . . ."

36

Dominique laughed softly. She touched my cheek with her fingers, stroking lightly. "Yes, I know how I must have looked. But you don't know how you looked . . . with your gown open . . ." She sighed contentedly, her warm hand moving to touch my breast.

"But then you changed! You ordered me to come to dinner, the way you'd speak to a slave, and I wanted to strike you! I would have, too, except I had no place to go afterwards." I heard the sharp intake of Dominique's breath but I hushed her before she could speak. "So I pretended to be bored with you and with your home because it was the only way I could express my anger . . . and my hurt."

"And you did it beautifully, love. Yesterday I had decided to tell you . . ."

I had to interrupt. "Wait, let me finish before I forget what I'm saying." Dominique's fingers were moving, lightly circling, and I felt my flesh swell under that delicate touch.

"I was dreaming of you when you came into the room last night. I remember reaching for you, wanting to continue the dream and so I . . ." Dominique's hand moved slowly down my body. "So I was embarrassed this morning and afraid of what you may have decided to do. You could send me away, you know. And I was ashamed, too, until I remembered that it took both of us to do what we did and that you had come to me . . ." I had to stop. Dominique's mouth covered mine. Her tongue entered and in the soft, wet darkness, my tongue met hers.

Was that sufficient explanation? I wanted her to understand that I felt no regret, that my only fear had been that she would.

37

And where had she gotten the tea?

I moved my legs apart to give her entrance.

I heard her quickened breath and the little wet noises of her mouth on my flesh.

"Wider!"

I obeyed. I felt her slip inside me. It caused a pleasure so close to pain that I gasped, and gasped again. We began a motion remembered from the night — Dominique giving, I receiving, point and counterpoint. We would thrust toward each other, meet, then move slowly apart only to rush together again as if our flesh could not bear the separation. Dominique was within me when, all too soon, the pleasure burst, carrying fire through my veins. I held her, imprisoned between my thighs, until I regained control of my breathing, until my sight cleared.

I looked up into green eyes. Her face was flushed, her expression loving, but there was an underlay of . . . something. What was this that I saw, that I sensed beneath the triumph in her smile?

"Dommie?"

She smiled at her new name.

"Dommie, what were you going to tell me yesterday?"

"Oh, love, it's not important. What I feared didn't take place so there's no need to tell you now." She kissed me lightly on the lips then took her place at my side. I pulled the sheet to her shoulder and tucked it around her. I was not to be put off. I wanted to know where she rode last night and all those other nights, with whom she rode and what it was that gave her fear.

So I said, "Whatever it was, it could have caused me to leave here. And if I had left . . ."

38

"Think of what we'd have missed." Dominique, obviously not intending to discuss the subject further, raised herself on an elbow to give me a sample of the kind of kiss we would have missed. A narrow ray of sunlight, escaping into the room through a misaligned shutter, clearly showed her face to me. I realized then that it was full daylight. The morning was far advanced and we were still abed.

"Dommie, we have to get dressed . . . now!" I pushed back the sheet and swung my feet over the side of the bed.

"Why? I like you better this way."

"No! The servants will be here to straighten the room. Please, we have to get up!"

I was half out of the bed before Dominique pulled me back, both of her arms around me, her cheek against my bare shoulder. "I took care of that long ago, love. When I went down to get your tea I told Malissa that we were both very tired and wouldn't want to be disturbed. No one will come near unless we ring."

I knew this to be true. I had found this household geared only and entirely to Dommie's comfort. She was served quietly and efficiently, her needs anticipated; no one would climb the stairs unless called.

"In that case I know what I'd like to do."

"What?" The gold flecks in Dommie's eyes sparkled in the light, the green deepened. She knew, as well as I, what it was we both wanted.

* * * * *

39

The next days were like none I had ever experienced in all of my life before Dominique. Many times I had felt happiness but those moments paled to nothingness when compared to the brightness, the glow which existed within me now.

What would my father have thought about me now? Would he have condemned my love for Dominique as "unnatural"? It didn't seem unnatural to me and so I did not spend time searching for an answer I might not wish to hear.

There was, however, one question I asked frequently; it was also frequently asked of me.

"Do you love me?"

Dominique and I would ask this of each other while walking in the garden or during sunlit rides on the river bank. We asked this at the dinner table, when the room held naught but the two of us, or during our evenings in the library as we watched the hands of the clock move with agonizing slowness towards a respectable bedtime.

Often I was willing to go directly to bed after the evening meal. There were, in fact, times I would have willingly foregone the meal.

In bed Dommie would whisper, "Do you love me?" and expect my answer at a time when I was incapable of understandable speech.

I, for one, could not manage even a few minutes that I did not think of Dommie and bed. My body would pulse when I brought to mind the feeling of her hands and mouth moving over my willing, naked flesh. Then I would think of her face, beautiful in sweet surrender, and her white thighs, parted, inviting my touch. Ahhh.

I could not get enough of her, nor she of me. During the day, and for the sake of propriety, we tried to maintain a suitable distance if there was a chance of being observed for this house was full of servants who moved freely throughout the rooms. Dominique solved our problem.

Far in the woods there was an abandoned wooden shack, partially destroyed by the elements but with an almost intact brick chimney and a sagging roof covering part of one room. This was our hideaway. We would eat our lunch from the basket of food Malissa supplied, sip wine from crystal goblets, lie together on a quilt and make love.

The moment we dismounted I was ready to undress but Dommie would tease, "Maybe you aren't ready enough, love," and she'd unbutton her shirt, opening it to reveal her smooth breasts. I would reach but she would pull back, "Are these what you want?" she'd ask innocently, her hands uplifting those soft mounds, raising and offering them. Often she would make me wait, undressing completely, then posing, her long hair concealing shoulders and breasts. I would kneel and wait for her to move to me so that I could enclose her hips with my arms, touch the black tangle of hair with my lips, move my tongue down the fold of her legs, stopping where that sweet triangle ended. Very soon, my own excitement beyond enduring, I would bear her to the ground and there, in dappled sunlight as the branches overhead answered to the wind, she would open herself fully, would give her body and her love to me.

I had not thought of myself as a sentimental person, a person to be ruled by the feelings in my heart, but I learned in those days, to my great surprise, that my heart is entirely capable of directing my every emotion, my every thought, every action; and it can do this in a way independent of whatever common sense I possess.

I am governess to Dommie's children, which makes Dommie my mistress . . . and my heart grins when I use this term, defined in the manner which was intended. I am now poor; not destitute but without funds to completely support myself, and Dommie owns a huge home and vast acres, a negotiable fortune. Dommie is a matron of approaching middle years, I am old to be a virgin but still considered young. There may even be regional differences in our outlook, North versus South, but these have not been apparent. I could probably think of many reasons why love between us is impossible; not the least being that we are both women. I could . . . but I don't.

My eyes, which had been closed for long minutes, opened to see the oak branches in silhouette overhead, the weathered shingles, sunlight streaming through splintered boards, Dommie's face above mine shadowing the sun from my eyes. My body stilled, my heart smiled. She questioned, "Do you want more, little girl?"

I answered, as she knew I would, "Yes, more."

CHAPTER VI
August, 1862

"I won't be with you tonight, love."

I knew this would happen someday . . . Dommie's night rides had been curtailed since we became lovers. We had been together every night since that first time in my room but I knew she would return to whatever it was that she did . . . and the time had come.

"Why?"

"I have to go out . . ."

"Dommie, I'm not a child. I believe I have a right to know where you go, with whom and why . . . I don't think that's too much to ask!"

We were at breakfast. She stared at the table for a moment then shrugged. "I don't think . . ."

I interrupted, "I love you Dommie. I mean it when I say it. And that gives me the right to know what it is you're doing that takes you away from me."

Dommie sighed and placed her napkin on the table. We both stood. "Come to the library," she said, "We'll talk there."

I followed her across the hall and into the library and waited while she closed the door. We did not embrace, we did not even touch. She led me to the leather-backed seat then took a chair opposite.

"I don't know how to begin," she said.

"Well, just tell me where you go and why. That'll be a good start."

She sighed and stared out of the window behind me. The morning sun was bright on her face, I could see the tiny frown as she tried to find a way to begin. Finally, her eyes looking into mine, she said simply, "I escort escaped slaves north towards the state line to Kentucky."

"You what?" I almost screamed.

"Yes." Her voice was calm. "I follow certain trails or the rail line until I reach a place where other people take over. Sometimes there's no one waiting at the nearest point so I have to go farther . . . until I can turn them over to someone."

"You and Hank do this?" I could not believe what I was hearing.

She nodded, "Yes. Sometimes Henry, too. We give them food, clothing, papers, whatever's needed, so that they can pass along the line."

I had sensed all along that it was something illegal. If your activities are aboveboard, you don't have to ride like a thief through the night . . . you transact whatever it is during daylight hours. It occurred to me that I now had the answers to some questions I hadn't asked.

"You keep some of them here in the house, don't you?" I was remembering the new faces I saw constantly — particularly the young woman who had done my hair so competently the night of the dinner party.

She nodded, "Yes. If they were house slaves we can do that. And we hide a few at a time in the compound to rest where it's safe. Malissa decides."

I looked at this remarkable woman whom I loved with all my heart. I wanted to take her in my arms. But we weren't finished yet.

"Why are you gone more than one night sometimes? I remember that you were away once for two days and three nights!"

"Because we can't travel in daylight. It's only safe at night when we can disappear into the darkness if we're being chased. We have to hide from the soldiers, too, you see."

"This is the reason you sent Elsas and Antoinette to New Orleans, isn't it?" I knew this was so.

"Yes, to keep them from harm if we're found out. I feel very strongly about what I'm doing. I don't want to stop."

"Was it this that you started to tell me at the table that day . . . before you stomped out of the room?"

She nodded. "Yes. We thought we'd been . . . betrayed, that a trap had been set for us. I was going to ask you to stay and help take care of Elsas and Antoinette if I got killed. I was so afraid that day . . . I thought it was going to be my last and I had such . . . such strong feelings for you . . . feelings that I couldn't get sorted in my mind." She reached to take my hands. "But it was a false alarm, nothing happened and I was so relieved to be home safe that I ran to your room." She smiled, remembering that night. "And there you were on that tiny sofa and I was thinking of our kiss the night of the party . . ." She shrugged lightly, smiling. "I just couldn't help myself . . ."

Ha! She was about as defenseless as a mountain cougar.

I was not to be put off. "Dommie, you realize you could get killed?"

She nodded. "Yes, we've been shot at a few times."

Now I could say it. "I'm riding with you tonight."

"No! No, I won't have that!"

"I would rather be killed with you than have you killed without me! I'm going with you tonight!"

Dommie was unreasonably stubborn. I had found her to be a gentle, considerate lover, a passionate lover. No erotic dream could describe the fulfillment I found in her arms; her touch aroused desire so fierce that I had trouble breathing. Nor could my senses have imagined the satisfaction in awakening passion in her. But she was, in this case, more stubborn than the meanest mule that ever lived.

"Are we having our first argument?" I was not above appealing to her regard for our love, so new, so precious.

"No, it takes two to argue and I'm leaving."

I walked with her to the door, placing myself between it and her. "Won't you change your mind?" I twined my arms around her neck and lightly touched my lips to hers. "If you don't, I'll follow you anyway."

"No you won't."

Did I detect a slightly less severe tone? I kissed her again, this time with my mouth open on hers. She responded as I knew she would. I moved my arms down her back, pulling her to me as I leaned against the door. We kissed, and kissed more.

With or without approval, I knew that I would ride with her. I am stubborn, too.

She leaned away, took my face in her hands and for a long moment looked at me lovingly, as if committing my features to memory. Then she pressed her mouth to mine again; our tongues meeting, moving together, tasting each other's sweetness. I felt a surge of wetness between my legs. When we parted in order to breathe she whispered, "Let's go upstairs, little girl."

I reached behind to turn the knob, my fingers unsteady. I very much wanted to be with her in bed. I opened the door and we moved sedately towards the stairs. There was no one in sight; our pace quickened. As we opened Dommie's bedroom door, it being nearest, she paused and said sweetly, "The answer is still no."

* * * * *

I couldn't read, I couldn't sleep, but I could pace. And I did. Then I turned my armchair towards the window and sat, peering into the night, my ears straining for the sound of horses.

I had been ready to go with her. I was even dressed in my riding clothes. I had thought there was no power on earth that could stop me from riding at her side, short of physical restraint, that is. But there was something to stop me, after all. Seeing me, Dommie's eyes had brimmed with tears. "Please, Faith, please don't!" The tears spilled. She embraced me and I heard, "Please, I love you so much . . . please don't!"

I sighed. She knows what she's doing, I thought, but she could make a mistake trying to keep me safe. She could be hurt trying to protect me. She doesn't know yet that I can handle myself. I had sighed again, "All right. I'll stay."

Staring out into blackness, listening, I thought of how easily I had been turned from my intention. Love imposes a few restrictions. Her anger would not have moved me but I could not long bear the sight of that proud, strong woman begging, her eyes filled with helpless tears.

After many hours I fell asleep.

* * * * *

I came awake as the door opened.

Dommie knelt in front of me, put her arms around my hips and her head in my lap. "I'm home, little girl."

"Are you all right?" I peered down at her, my hands touching her shoulders. Then I realized the significance of the light coming in the windows. "Oh, no, Dommie! It's daylight!"

"Well, yes . . ." she said reasonably, smiling up at me, her face tired, smudged.

"You rode in daylight? You're not supposed to ride in daylight!" Remembering her reason for not riding in daylight, I felt my heart lurch. "Why, baby, why?"

"I didn't want you to worry if I didn't come home." This was simply said and showed the depth of her love.

I stroked her hair. "Is this the way it's going to be from now on, Dommie? I sit and wait for you to be shot in the night or, failing that, I sit and wait for you to be shot in daylight because you don't want me to worry about your being shot at night? I don't think that's fair. I admire what you're doing and I'll share it with you, whatever the danger, but I won't spend my life in an agony of suspense, waiting to claim your body from some ditch. I don't see that I can do that."

"I won't put you in danger, Faith. I'll quit first."

* * * * *

Dommie was rested and full of energy. Also starved. We were at an early supper and she was eating everything in sight. I waited until the table was cleared and we had been served carrot cake and sweet tea.

"Do you remember this morning?" I asked, "what you said?"

49

"What I said about quitting?" Her memory was perfect. She knew what she'd said and why she'd said it.

"Yes. But, Dommie, I don't want you to stop doing what's important just to please me. It would be better if I rode with you." I had thought long and hard about this.

"No."

"What, then?"

"The banker you met at our dinner party, Sidney Graves, remember him?"

I nodded but I didn't really remember him. I would not have remembered the grim reaper if he had sat at my right hand . . . I only remembered Dommie and the taste of her lips.

"Sidney was my father's friend and he knows what we're doing and helps when he can. He's been telling me that I should quit. I've been at this for years and he says my time is running out. I think I believe him." She picked a few cake crumbs from the table, rolled them absently between her fingers.

"Sidney feels that I should leave, take Antoinette and Elsas somewhere, or stay in New Orleans . . . but leave here. He'll pay this year's cotton sales through his bank and, with what I have already, there'll be enough to last for years. If I want to sell this place he'll handle the legal part and pay me by draft wherever we decide to locate."

I listened intently, carefully following her words, searching her face for some sign, but could not read her expression.

"Dommie, would you want to do this?"

"I would, yes." She looked at me, put her hand out for me to grasp. "I have you to live for now. It's selfish, I know, but I want to live with you. I want the years that we have . . . I don't want to end up in a ditch, either, and I can't risk that happening to you. I love my children and I'll care for them as best I can but I want a life . . . with you."

I was happy as we made our plans. It would take some weeks but we were going to leave Nashville for New Orleans and then, perhaps, for some other place. Dommie would no longer be at risk.

That night as we lay side by side, Dommie's head on my arm, she talked about New Orleans. "I still have my grandparents' home on Saint Charles Avenue but it's leased for several more years so we'll stay in a hotel at first — the Saint Louis or the Saint Charles." Her foot rubbed against my leg. "Or, we might lease an apartment in the Pontalba Buildings. Would you like to live in the Vieux Carre?"

"Sure." I would have agreed to anything she suggested — living in a tent, a sod hogan, a hole in the ground — if that's what it took to be with her and keep her safe.

"You'll like the Saint Louis if we stay there. It's near the French Opera House, and the Pontalba buildings are on both sides of the Place d'Armes." She thought for a few seconds. "Except I think it's called Jackson Square now."

"If I remember, there's a war and New Orleans is under Union occupation. That might have something to do with where we stay, don't you think?"

"No, there'll be a place for us. I'll have Sidney take care of it once we decide." Sometimes I forgot that Dommie was a very wealthy woman, accustomed to having what she wanted, war or no.

51

As Dommie slept, cushioned against me, I marveled at the changes in my life. I had known that marriage wasn't for me but didn't have reason to back up the knowledge. And, at my father's death, I had despaired of ever having a home; I thought to spend my life alone. Now, at twenty-three, I had a home and, unexpectedly, I also had love. Coming late to physical passion, it seems, does not mean a diminishment of need. I wanted Dommie more and more . . . each kiss, each caress, built desire. I could not imagine life without her.

* * * * *

Dommie was adamant. I was to go alone by train to Memphis, taking the trunks. She and Malissa and Henry would travel by carriage and meet me there. This was a new plan, one in which I had not had a say, not even a warning of the change. I didn't understand why the four of us couldn't travel together. Finally, after refusing to travel at all unless I was given a good reason for setting out on my own, I was told that we were to travel separately in case anything happened. "You do remember that we're in the middle of a war, don't you?" I raised my eyebrows at this convenient reminder.

This way, Dommie told me sensibly, if we separated for those few days and if anything happened while either of us was en route, there would be someone left to look after Antoinette and Elsas. I didn't think her plan was any too well thought out but I finally agreed just to keep the peace.

"What will happen to the cotton?" I asked. "Who'll harvest it?" I knew that it would ripen in late September or October, after we were gone.

"Cotton is picked, love, not harvested, and there'll be pickers when the time comes. Hank takes care of that part and Sidney handles the sale."

"And the horses?" I was thinking about Spirit.

"Oh, they'll be sold." To be dismissed so casually, the horses must be last in Dommie's thoughts.

The arrangements for closing the house were left to Malissa. She had sufficient help so that, one by one, each room was cleaned and covered until we were almost living out of trunks.

I left Nashville on a Wednesday, after a tearful parting and, what with the inevitable delays, did not enter Memphis until two long days later. I could have walked faster.

Dommie was to meet me a day prior to boarding our river transportation, the *Memphis Queen*, but she did not arrive on Monday, nor had she appeared by Tuesday morning, the day of our scheduled departure for New Orleans. I was frantic and had no idea what I should do.

The *Memphis Queen* was to cast off in the late afternoon, so, deciding that I should follow Dommie's plan with or without her, I checked out of the hotel, had our trunks loaded aboard the ship and took possession of our stateroom. Then I waited.

At each sound I would rush to a window, peering at the wharf, trying to identify the source. I watched four horses and eight goats parade to containment on the lower deck, heard laborers curse as they manhandled heavy barrels fastened to the end of a sling, watched a crate come apart allowing red chickens to squawk their way into the river. Some flapped to the dock, chased enthusiastically by a horde of ragged children.

Later, as I peered through the window, I saw Henry lifting Dommie out of a hired carriage. Malissa, waiting, put an arm around Dommie's waist as Dommie slumped against her. For a moment I was paralyzed with fright. I rushed from the cabin, down the enclosed stairway and out across the narrow deck, only to see the three of them still huddled on the dock. Malissa and Henry were both supporting Dommie, whose face, even from a distance, was ashen, eyes closed. I flew down the passenger ramp.

"What's the matter? Dommie! What is it?" I bent to peer into her face, my hands gripping her arms. "Dommie?"

"She can't walk up the ramp." Malissa's arm was tight around Dommie's waist, her shoulder supporting Dommie's head.

"Why? What's wrong?" I asked this of Malissa because Dommie's mouth was pinched closed. She did not look as if she had the strength to speak.

"She can't walk," Malissa repeated.

I stared at Dommie, unable for the moment to take in what I heard. Was something wrong with her legs?

Malissa began to say it again, more firmly, "She can't . . ."

I interrupted, "Well, Henry can!" I looked up to meet his eyes. "Help her!"

Henry leaned and lifted Dommie easily, cradling her against his chest. I think Dommie fainted at that moment for the terrible strain left her face, and her

54

hand, dangling and limp, fell open to release the lacy cloth that had been balled in her clenched fingers.

Ignoring the many staring eyes and gaping mouths that followed our progress, I led the way to our cabin and stood aside for Henry to enter.

CHAPTER VII
August, 1862

Gently Henry lowered Dommie to the couch. Malissa was there with a pillow from the bed, placing it carefully under Dommie's head. Overcome by fear, I knelt and touched Dommie's cheek with mine. Dimly I was aware of the cabin door closing and, knowing we were now alone, I held her face in my hands and rained kisses on every inch of it.

Slowly Dommie's eyes opened and she smiled at me. It wasn't much of a smile but I was heartened by it. "Sweetheart, I'm all right. I'm just very tired." Her voice was no more than a whisper.

"You . . . you're all right? You're not sick?" I was incredulous. If not sick, what?

"I need to rest." Her smile faded and her eyes closed. She slept or, perhaps, fainted; her face was pale, her lips colorless.

"Kneeling there like that isn't going to help, Missy, we need to get those things off of her."

I stood, whirling, to look straight into green eyes that were on a level with my own. It came to me then that I had seldom looked directly at Malissa. Her face was usually turned away and her eyes downcast so I couldn't have noticed that she and Dommie shared not only the same eye coloring but the same shape, the same flecks of color that seemed to reflect light.

"You . . . you're . . ." I sputtered, unable to put my thoughts into words.

"Whatever you're thinking will wait. Now help me get these clothes off before she bleeds to death." Malissa's words were not those of a slave; she was giving me an order in a tone that brooked no refusal.

The meaning of her words suddenly sank in. My concern for Dommie overrode my shock. Imploring, I touched Malissa's arm. "What happened to her, what's wrong?"

"I don't know . . ." Malissa was working at the tiny buttons on Dommie's dress, her hands moving swiftly. "We need warm water. Henry's just outside the door, send him for some."

It did not occur to me to question this. I found Henry standing squarely in the middle of the passageway, his huge arms crossed, his feet firmly planted on the carpet. From his stance I doubted the entire Union Army could have budged him.

"Henry, we need warm water," I said without preamble.

His acknowledgement was a nod. He turned and moved swiftly down the corridor towards the stairway.

I closed the door and secured the latch then went to the couch and looked over Malissa's shoulder, cursing the helpless feeling that swept over me. Drawing a deep breath, I asked, "What can I do, Malissa?"

Her back still to me, she said, "Do you have night clothes or another dress in that bag?" She nodded towards my reticule still on the bed where I'd dropped it.

"Yes, I think so . . . yes, a gown."

"Well then, we'll cut this off . . . I can't get it unfastened." And she proceeded to slit the seams of Dommie's bodice with a knife she produced from somewhere beneath her apron. Gently she lifted the fabric, exposing a bloodied chemise.

"My God, what happened to her!"

Without answering, Malissa cut the seams, exposing Dommie from the waist up.

Horrified, I stared at Dommie's white shoulders and the heavy leather straps that were cutting into that smooth flesh.

"We're going to have to use these straps again. I'd better not cut them," Malissa said softly. "Help me get them off." She began to pull the leather over Dommie's shoulders.

Leaning, I maneuvered Dommie's arms so that Malissa could draw the straps down. We both ignored the soft moans as we moved Dommie this way and

58

that, Malissa touching as gently as possible but causing pain as she pulled on the blood-soaked leather.

"Put that shawl under her. We don't want blood on the couch."

This would not have occurred to me. I lifted Dommie's shawl from where it had fallen and, as Malissa gently pulled her upright, placed it under Dommie's back.

"Let's get the rest of this off." And Malissa slit and opened a skirt seam with the knife.

Dumfounded, I stared at little sacks that were tied to a web of leather around Dommie's hips. "What . . ." I sputtered, "what *ARE* they?"

"Gold," Malissa said, busy untying the thongs which held the sacks to the leather harness. "All gold."

"Gold?" I echoed. "Where did Dommie get so much gold?" There had to be more than a dozen sacks, each one clinking as Malissa dropped it to the carpet.

"That's not for me to say," she said. "She'll tell you when the time comes." Swiftly she slit Dommie's underclothing with the knife and pulled the fabric away.

My mind registered slim thighs, softly rounded hips, the triangle of black hair at the part of her legs, her bosom crossed with angry red welts where the straps had pressed.

Dommie moved her head; eyes closed, she whispered, "Faith, love . . ."

I felt my face flame and I looked at Malissa.

Malissa smiled and I saw kindness in her face. "Nothing for you to worry about, Missy. I've known about the two of you from the first."

Before I could form a reply, although I had no idea what I was going to say, we heard a knock. Thankful for the interruption, I crossed to the door. The soft knock sounded again. Henry!

After looking over my shoulder to see Malissa covering Dommie with a blanket from the bed, I undid the latch and opened the door.

Henry filled the entire opening. He held a pot of steaming water, his hands protected by heavy rags. I stood aside and he entered, his tread causing the floor to shake.

"Put that on the stand, Henry, and thank you." Malissa's smile would probably have been thank you enough. Henry looked at the couch then at Malissa.

Malissa walked to him and put her hand on his arm. Looking up she said, "She'll be fine, Henry, really."

Reassured, and with a swift glance at me, Henry moved to the door, closing it quietly behind him.

Malissa poured some of the steaming water into the wash basin then added cool water from the pitcher. She dampened the end of one of the towels provided for our use and began cleaning the raw wounds on Dommie's shoulders.

I dampened another towel and handed it to her when the one she was using was bloody. We worked like that, she sponging those white shoulders and I rinsing and wringing the towels, until the water in the basin was pink.

Henry took the basin to empty and returned it to us full of warm water.

"We're going to have to cut one of their towels," Malissa said. She proceeded to make squares of the thick, white linen and placed the clean cloths over the wounds. Then, using a towel I had rinsed in fresh water, she began to wipe away the rest of the blood and travel grime.

Together we managed to sit Dommie upright so that Malissa could wipe both her front and back, a job I would have relished if the circumstances had not been so frightful. I had a clean white gown in my reticule and we pulled this over Dommie's head, carefully holding the linen bandages in place on her shoulders.

Dommie stirred as we manipulated her on the couch but did not quite awaken from the stuporous sleep into which she had fallen. Malissa and I managed to move her to one of the beds and we both sighed with relief when Dommie shifted position then began snoring gently, her face still pale but now somewhat relaxed. Throughout, Dommie had not moved her arms; the pain from her wounded shoulders must have been unbearable in spite of her almost unconscious state.

We had been concentrating entirely upon Dommie but now I became aware of sounds and movements outside the cabin. I walked to the window opening and looked out just in time to see the passenger gangplank raised.

"We'll be on our way very soon, Malissa," I said.

Malissa nodded. "I think we'd better clean our mess, Faith, I have a feeling we're going to have company." This was the first time Malissa had spoken my name.

Hurriedly, we picked up the shredded clothing and the soiled linen, packing all of this out of sight in a bureau drawer. The gold was another matter.

"Malissa, there must be over fifty pounds of gold in these sacks! How in the world did she ever manage to carry it?" Then a thought struck me, "Why didn't you or Henry help her?" I knew that Henry could have easily carried a horse under one arm.

"Nobody," Malissa explained, "not even a runaway soldier, is going to search a lady, but Henry could have been conscripted on the spot and a black woman is fair game for any man these days; Dominique was the only one who could safely get the gold through."

"How long has she carried it?"

Malissa paused to count. "She's carried it for the five days we've been on the road. Yesterday and most of today on foot." She looked at me and continued sadly, "Spirit was killed when some men held us up and took the horses and our luggage. They wanted Spirit, too, but Dominique shot at them and one of them shot Spirit." Malissa shook her head. "I don't ever remember her being so sad. She hardly spoke for the rest of the time. She just walked and cried and there wasn't anything we could do to help her."

I felt tears fill my eyes; I had loved Spirit, too.

Malissa draped my shawl around my shoulders. "Now we're ready for company."

We heard men's voices in the corridor then a soft tap on the door. I clutched the shawl tighter around me and said, in a voice just loud enough to be heard, "Coming."

It was, as Malissa suspected, the captain. I opened the door wide enough for him to get a glimpse of Dommie, obviously asleep, obviously ill. Not so obvious was the gold under the mattress. "My dear Captain, how kind of you to call." I slipped through the half-opened door and closed it behind me.

"Ma'am, there is still time to take the lady ashore if you wish. We'll be casting off within the hour and, as you know, it will be overnight until the next berth."

Dommie's unusual method of boarding had been reported to him, it seemed. Well, what of it? "You are very considerate, sir, but I think Mrs. LeCompte needs rest more than anything else."

"If there's anything you need, Ma'am, don't hesitate to ask."

"We'll require bedding for our maid, Captain, and a simple meal for the three of us . . ."

Back in the room, I shut the door and leaned my back against it; I was undecided whether to laugh or cry with relief.

The decision was taken from me by the ungodly sound of the ship's whistle, apparently housed directly overhead, which caused Dommie to awaken in a fright. I rushed to her side, unmindful of Malissa, and soothed her with soft kisses until she sank back into a deep slumber.

* * * * *

True to the captain's word, bed linen and a tray of soup, hot tea, and fresh rolls fragrant and steaming, was delivered to us before we were away from the dock. Wonder about our delayed departure was answered as we ate. There was some commotion out of sight from our cabin, loud voices in angry dispute, then the gangway was lowered to allow a party of men to board.

"Malissa," I asked between bites, "those men wouldn't have anything to do with us, would they?" I knew with certainty that the gold had not been in Dommie's possession when I saw her last. Gold, in the considerable amount under our mattress, would leave some trace.

Malissa buttered a roll, then spoke. "Maybe, maybe not." She shrugged.

I knew I would have to tread lightly. "If we are to be questioned about anything I must know enough to give plausible answers. I'm not asking you to betray Dommie, surely you know that?"

Malissa looked at me, her face serious. "There may be . . . trouble . . . but Dominique will be the one to tell you." She pushed back her chair. "If you're finished I'll have Henry take the tray and I'll go with him to see that he has a place to sleep and some food. You'll take care of Dominique while I'm gone?"

I heard Malissa laugh for the first time as I said lightly, "Maybe, maybe not."

As soon as I had locked the door behind her, I went to the bed and sat on the edge next to Dommie's sleeping form. She was on her back, arms by her side, breathing deeply. I bent to kiss those pale lips, knowing in my heart that I would stand with her against the world.

Eventually, there was a great creaking and splashing, the boat shuddering and groaning as it departed the dock, the whistle screaming without end.

I stood at the window, watching the shore move past, until it was too dark to see. Malissa had returned and was on the sofa, arms folded, head nodding, and it wasn't until then that I realized how exhausted she must be.

Early in the night Dommie woke in pain and, we thought, light-headed from hunger. Malissa, still resting on the sofa, was up in an instant. "The towels are stuck to her skin and she needs food. Lock the door after me." She was gone before I could say a word.

I had been lying, fully dressed, on the other bed. At Malissa's words I rose, locked the door, then returned to sit by Dommie. I don't think she was fully aware of my presence until I adjusted the sheet around her shoulders.

"Faith?" Her eyes were closed, her face flushed.

"Yes, Dommie, I'm here." I took her hand in mine and leaned to kiss her forehead. Her flesh was hot to my touch.

"Did Malissa tell you?"

I was not sure what she meant. "Tell me what, darling?"

Dommie's eyes opened, brimming bright with tears. "Spirit's dead! They took everything then they shot him and I had to . . . I had to kill him, Faith. I was bringing him for you and now he's dead . . ." She began to cry, great heartbroken sobs that tore at me until, helpless to ease her pain, I began to cry, too. I held her then, unmindful of her poor shoulders, and we cried together.

Sometime later a few spoonfuls of warm soup and tea seemed to give strength to Dommie's tearful smile. I fed her spoon by spoon and told myself I could see improvement with each swallow.

Malissa soaked the bloodstained cloths from Dommie's shoulders and put fresh linen on the wounds and Dommie was asleep again before we straightened the bed covering. I was thankful that the blood had stopped oozing from the deep gashes but alarmed because Dommie's body felt very hot and her face was burning. We put a damp cloth on her forehead to ease the heat but Dommie was asleep and past noticing what we did for her. I was afraid that the constant rumble of the ship's wheel would disturb her but she didn't seem to hear.

Malissa returned to the sofa, I turned down the lamp and lay once more on my bed. Staring up at the ceiling, feeling the steady throb of the engine, I wondered how long it would be before I could hold Dommie in my arms, soothing her hurt, kissing away the pain of Spirit's death. As I drifted into sleep, my imagination pictured those things we did when in bed. My last thought was of Dommie's silken hair falling on my face and shoulders as she pressed her breasts to mine.

CHAPTER VIII
August, 1862

Near dawn. I was awakened by the sound of someone retching. I pushed myself upright in time to see Henry opening the cabin door, a covered chamber pot in one huge hand. I threw back the light blanket covering my legs and knew, before I scrambled from the bed, that Dommie had not recovered during the night. There was an odor of bile, a sickening smell that told of nausea and an illness far more serious than torn shoulders.

Malissa, sitting on the edge of Dommie's bed, was gently wiping Dommie's face with a damp cloth. She looked up when I touched her arm.

"She woke thirsty and I tried giving her some tea and that seemed to start it. She can't hold anything down." Malissa turned back to Dommie. "I don't know what to do . . ."

It did not take more than one look at Dommie's face, even in the dim light from the lamp, for me to realize that I didn't know what to do either. There was no color in her cheeks; her lips were pale, her eyelids and the tender flesh beneath them purplish in color. Her lips were slightly parted and, except for each labored breath, she lay as still as death.

I snatched my shawl from the chair. "I'm going to get the doctor, Malissa, he'll know what to do." I spoke confidently in order to reassure both of us. I had my hand on the door knob, the shawl still dragging the floor, when Malissa half whispered, "There is no doctor. I already tried."

I turned to her and snapped accusingly, "There has to be a doctor. All boats have doctors!" This statement may or may not have been true but I spoke with the hope of desperation.

"Not this one. Haven't you noticed that we aren't moving? Soldiers have been swarming all over the place since we stopped a while ago." Before I could speak, she added, "Whatever's going on isn't good." She folded the cloth and tenderly placed it across Dommie's forehead. Then she sat as still as stone, hands clasping each other, head bowed. I couldn't tell if she was praying or sleeping or just looking at Dommie.

I try to be patient, always, but it is simply not in my nature to sit with bowed head.

"Malissa, we can't just let her lie there! I know the captain keeps medicines for emergencies and I'll go fetch whatever he has." I was almost out the door this time before she stopped me.

"No! Don't you go out there! The soldiers arrested the captain when they got on and Henry saw them shoot somebody. You start roaming around and they'll likely arrest you, too. Or," she added grimly, "They'll do even worse."

This caught me up short. I had no wish to be raped. Not by soldiers or, for that matter, by anyone else. Quietly I closed the door.

Almost immediately there was a soft knock which I knew to be Henry's. He brought the chamber pot, rinsed and clean, and a pail filled with water, and was none too soon with both of them for Dommie was sick again.

Twice more within the hour Henry had to empty both containers. As busy as we were, we could not fail to hear the loud, angry voices in the corridor and on the deck, and once the sound of several shots. I was not frightened by any of this. Nothing that took place on the other side of our door was of any importance to me.

Dommie was dying. She was too ill to know either of us and her only sound was the terrible, convulsive retching that, by then, produced only thin strings of bile. I held her as the spasms racked her body but I could not know if this was comfort to her. What I did know was that her strength, that magnificent courage she used so freely for others, was gone and she could fight for herself no longer.

69

"I'm going for help, Malissa." I rose and straightened my gown, unmindful of the stains, some wet, some dry, that spattered the bodice. My arms were leaden as I arranged my shawl.

Malissa looked up and nodded dully.

I opened the door, only mildly surprised to find a blue-coated soldier standing in the opening, a rifle cradled in his arms. "You're not supposed to leave, Ma'am," he said, not unkindly.

"My cousin is dying. I need medical help." Was this the voluble Faith speaking? Heartbreak had sheared my vocabulary to the bone. I stood mute, waiting for this young man to give me leave but knowing that, with or without it, I was going to find something to make Dommie well.

The young man stepped into the doorway and closed the door. "I know she's sick, Ma'am, I've been hearin' her for a while. My ma had that kind of sickness once but not as bad as your lady." He motioned to the stairway. "You go 'head of me there and we'll find the Lieutenant. They's bound to be some doctorin' somewhere on this boat."

It was only as we moved down the carpeted corridor that I realized how clean and sweet the air was outside our room. Malissa had been afraid to open the windows and, since they were our only source of fresh air, the room smelled heavily of sickness — the same odor clinging to my gown, I supposed.

I saw only a few soldiers lounging idly here and there. They watched as I passed but made no rude remarks that I heard.

We found the lieutenant in what I believe was the captain's chart room, bent over a map that was

70

spread on a slanted table. He looked up as we entered and straightened to return my soldier's salute, then said courteously and with a slight bow, "Lieutenant Barker at your service, Ma'am."

"My cousin is dying, Lieutenant. I need medical help." I now knew the fewer words the better. What I wanted was action not conversation.

"Yes, Ma'am, the captain told me that the lady was sick but there's no doctor aboard."

"Don't you have a medical person in your command? Surely someone ministers to your ill or wounded."

"We're a very small company, only enough of us to secure this ship."

I sighed. "Then show me, please, the medical supplies that were aboard when you took the ship."

He looked blank.

"Surely the ship's officers had things for emergencies! They have to be stored around here someplace."

This was obviously his first command. He remained blank.

"Well, is the ship's captain or some other ship's officer still aboard?" My urge was to shake him until his teeth rattled but I controlled the impulse and spoke calmly, as to a child. "If one is, we could ask, couldn't we?"

This the young man could handle. Perhaps he was not accustomed to dealing with women. "Soldier," he addressed my guard, "take the lady to Captain Hansen but don't let him out. They can talk through the door." He turned to me, "I'm sorry about your cousin, Ma'am, but tomorrow you'll have to go ashore. The other passengers were sent off earlier but

71

Captain Hansen persuaded me to let you stay. You see, we've found contraband aboard so we're confiscating this ship. All civilians have to go."

"Go?" I echoed dumbly. "Go where?"

Embarrassed, he shook his head and shrugged, not inclined to discuss my problem. He gave me a brief salute and turned to bend to his precious map again.

My guard led me down stairways and through impossibly narrow passageways until we finally arrived at what must have been the very bottom of the ship; there was water sloshing over the slatted wooden walkway, and tiny, cramped doors on either side. We stopped at one door that was secured with a padlock, newly installed, from the look of it. My young man's knock was answered by a voice I recognized.

"Captain Hansen, my cousin has become desperately ill. Please tell me where you keep the medical supplies and what I should give her." I forgot to announce my name but the good captain knew me and my errand at once.

"Under the bunk in my cabin. Metal box. Key in the desk drawer with a label." When necessary, he was a man of few words, too. "What are her symptoms?"

I wanted to run to his cabin. Time was precious, but I also needed to know which medicine to use. "She had fever, her stomach and bowels have emptied . . . she can't swallow and has . . . has been unconscious since daybreak." My voice choked, I knew I was describing death.

"Does she . . . was there blood?"

"Yes, some. Towards the last."

There was a long pause. I waited.

"Laudanum, I suppose might help." Another pause, "I think you have to make her drink whatever she can. Tea, water, diluted brandy, any liquid she can keep down will be good." Pause again. "Yes, and some laudanum. Two spoonfuls now and more later. Help her sleep, calm her stomach."

"Bless you, Captain," I called over my shoulder as I ran, stumbling towards the stairway, my hem wet and dragging.

The captain's word was good. We found the box, the key, the laudanum, a tot of brandy in a green bottle and in minutes I was back in our stateroom to see Malissa slumped on the chair, her head bowed, and Dommie lying silent and so very, very still. My heart stopped.

As I crossed the room I heard the door close quietly behind me and the key snap in the lock. We were prisoners again but nothing that could possibly happen in this world would matter to me now. I stood by the bedside, breathing the foul odor of death, looking at the ghostly whiteness of Dommie's face. Then I knelt and leaned to put my cheek against her cold one, hugging her to me. "Please, no!" I begged. "Please, no!"

Malissa touched me. "Did you get medicine?" Her fingers pinched my shoulder.

"Yes!" I hissed. "Yes!" Not that it made any difference.

"Well, let's give it to her!"

It took a second or two for her words to penetrate. My heart began beating again. I raised my head and saw that Dommie was breathing. Tears streaming, I rushed through the captain's instructions, found a spoon on Dommie's tray while Malissa added a tiny bit of brandy to a cup of water.

Dommie gagged and choked but we had no mercy. A spoonful at a time, we fed her water.

Thinking the liquid would go down better if Dommie could be raised a little, I sat at the head of the bed and we lifted her so that I could pillow her against me. Malissa sat next to the bed with the water glass and spoon and we managed to get Dommie to swallow almost a cupful. Then we gave her laudanum diluted with more water.

The minutes had passed slowly. Each drop of liquid that Dommie swallowed and retained seemed a major victory for Malissa and me. I breathed words of encouragement and praise in Dommie's ear. I do not know if she heard me or, if hearing, she tried a little harder but I know that holding her to my breast was comfort to me. Her slender back lay soft against me, her head rested on my shoulder and my arms enclosed her. I could touch my cheek to her hair and my lips waited to form the whispered words of love that I wanted her to hear if she returned to me from the dark place that had claimed her.

Dommie slept, her skin clammy, her breathing deeper, labored but without the long pauses between each breath. The laudanum, maybe? Or had sickness run its course?

My arms cramped so we lowered Dommie to the bed and I stood and stretched, watching to see that moving her had not worsened her condition. I believe that Malissa then saw in my face the same hope that I saw in hers.

I also saw how desperately tired Malissa had become. I counted what rest she had had since coming aboard and discovered that she had not slept, really slept, more than a few hours in what must have been three days, at the least.

"Malissa, I think you can rest now. You're no good to Dommie if you drop. Please, lie down. You don't have to sleep if you don't wish but you must rest. Please, Malissa."

I think that she was asleep before I untangled the blanket from where I had thrown it earlier this morning. I covered her, then stood looking at her sleeping face. It was there, the resemblance. Malissa's high cheekbones matched Dommie's. They shared the same facial features. Except for the coloring they could be sisters. How could I have failed to notice this? I had been with both of them for many weeks but had seen nothing.

The words mulatto and quadroon sprang to my mind, and tales of Southern men dallying with their female slaves. Malissa must be the product of such a union. Could she and Dommie have lineage in common? Had Dommie's father also fathered Malissa? My thoughts were jumbled and I could not sort out how or what I felt.

Right this minute, however, there were more important things than Malissa's parentage. First, I pushed aside the drapes and opened both windows, not worried that the light would awaken either Malissa or Dommie, but sure that the fresh, clean air would be beneficial to us all. Next, food. Neither Malissa nor I had eaten since yesterday and I deduced from the height of the sun that it was well into the afternoon. I was hungry.

Where was Henry? Was it possible that the Lieutenant felt Henry was a threat simply because of his size? If so, what had the soldiers done with him? Was he, too, locked in a tiny cell? I had to find him.

I did not want to leave Dommie's side for an instant but I must look to tomorrow. I went to her and bent to kiss her forehead. She did not stir. I smoothed my gown, more by reflex than by intention since I did not care about the wrinkles or the odor, then I rearranged a few loose strands of hair and, with a last look at Dommie, moved to the door.

CHAPTER IX
August, 1862

My young man was sitting on a straight-back chair, his rifle leaning against the wall. He rose as I stepped into the corridor, straightened his rumpled blue coat and half-way came to attention. "Is your lady any better, Ma'am?"

"I'm not certain but we hope so." His face held an expression of genuine concern so I added, "Thanks to your help."

"I was glad to do something, Ma'am. I just wish somebody could have helped my ma when she had the flux."

"She didn't recover?"

"No, Ma'am, she didn't. My whole family had it all at once but we all got better, all except her. It was funny 'cause she didn't have it as bad as the rest of us." He shrugged to signify, I imagine, that these things were past human understanding.

I put my hand on his arm. "Would you help us again?"

"Yes, Ma'am, I would." He was so very young and serious.

"My maid and I need something to eat and I'd like to have some broth for my cousin. We need to build her strength."

"We had rations a while ago and I know they's some left. I can fetch some for you. I think maybe they forgot you was here."

"Could you escort me to your Lieutenant first?" When he looked doubtful I added, "You heard that we're going to be put ashore? Well, I need to learn a little about that before we're actually shoved over the side."

He smiled. "They ain't going to do that, Ma'am."

"Whatever they're going to do, I need to know about it first." I touched his arm again. "Please?"

We found the Lieutenant at the top of the ship, in the glass-enclosed room where the steering was done, arguing with a freed Captain Hansen.

"Yes, Miss?" Lieutenant Barker seemed relieved to see me.

"How is your cousin?" Captain Hansen interrupted.

I smiled at them both. "Thanks to you gentlemen, I believe she is somewhat improved. Now may I impose on your kindness, Lieutenant, and ask specifically where we are to be put ashore, which city?"

The Lieutenant seemed about to answer, then hesitated, frowning.

I added respectfully, "If your destination is a military secret, of course I'll understand. It's just that my cousin is gravely ill and knowing our destination would greatly relieve my mind. I must insure her continued improvement . . ." I let my voice trail off, hoping he would not ask what one thing had to do with the other.

"Certainly, you must see to her comfort. Understand that I would not disturb her sickbed if not for my explicit instructions concerning civilians." He spoke sharply to my guard. "Soldier, escort the lady back to her cabin and see to it that she is provided with whatever she needs."

"Sir!" my young man barked.

I had not learned where we were to be landed but I murmured thanks and turned as if to go, then, seemingly as an afterthought, turned back. "Oh, Lieutenant, one more thing. Our servant, Henry, seems to have disappeared and we need him for certain sickroom tasks. Where will I find him?" Pray the young officer would find it hard to deny this innocent need.

The Lieutenant hesitated, then, "He's locked up below. I'll send word for him to be released immediately."

I was almost running by the time I reached our corridor, my guard close behind, his boots clumping on the deck as he tried to keep up. It took all of the patience I could muster to wait for him to find the key and unlock our door. Hardly hearing what he said about bringing food, I swept past him, my eyes on Dommie.

I looked down at her from the bedside, reassured to see that she was still breathing.

"Faith?" Dommie's voice was hardly more than a breath. I would swear that I heard her more with my heart than with my ears. I took her hand in both of mine and felt a slight pressure from her fingers. Her eyes still closed she said again, "Faith?"

I had thought never to hear her voice again. Tears filled my eyes and spilled on her hand as I kissed each finger. "I'm here, Dommie, I'm here, love." The slight pressure of her hand told me that she was awake and aware, if only dimly.

We stayed like that for long minutes until I heard a soft tapping on the door. I kissed her forehead then rose to open the door for Henry. He had lost his black coat, his shirt was soiled, the front pocket torn and hanging and his expression was not as imperturbable as usual. I saw his eyes move from Dommie to Malissa and then he looked at me, questioning.

"They're both sleeping, Henry. I think Dominique is getting better and Malissa is just resting. Come in, now, we'd better keep you out of sight."

Henry went immediately to Malissa's side. She was sleeping soundly but within seconds her eyes opened, almost as if she'd heard an unspoken command. She looked up and reached out her hand.

"I'm glad Faith got you out of that tiny room. We'll have food for you soon." Her expression was one of love, her smile gentle.

It occurred to me that Malissa did not know of my effort to rescue Henry or where he had been. Nor could she have had any inkling that food was on the way. I was tempted to ask how she knew things that she had no way of knowing but I held my tongue.

The food Malissa predicted was delivered by our young guard. It was a kind of stew, lukewarm, with meat, onions, and many potatoes in a thick, brown gravy. Large hunks of bread accompanied the pail of stew and there was a pitcher of water, a gob of melting lard and, in a small bowl, soup of the kind we had been served yesterday.

"Our benefactor brought only two plates, Malissa. You and Henry eat while I feed Dommie."

With Malissa's help, I raised Dommie on pillows then settled myself on the chair next to the bed. The soup was mostly broth but it was just right for swallowing I thought. Dommie thought otherwise.

No," she moaned as I touched her lips with the spoon. "No."

"You have to eat, love. We want you to get well." Again I held the spoon to her mouth. With surprising swiftness, considering her wounded shoulders and obvious weakness, she knocked the spoon from my hand.

"Dommie!"

I was not as indignant as I sounded. I leaned to pick up the spoon and, as I straightened, I saw Malissa smile. "The lady is better, wouldn't you say?" I asked quietly. Henry nodded.

Thinking to reason with her, I began, "Now, Dommie . . ."

She turned her face to the wall.

"That won't do you a bit of good. You have to drink this soup."

I heard a tiny "No."

Lightly stroking her face, I tried again. "You won't get well if you don't eat. Please, one spoonful?"

The barest of whispers, "I don't think I can."

I won't say that it was a pleasant meal for either of us. Of course, I did not stop at one spoonful, nor had I intended to. My poor darling tried but the liquid wouldn't always go down. She spewed soup over the front of her gown, the bedclothes, over my bosom and lap. She coughed it in every direction but, even so, managed to swallow some of the bowl's contents. We were both exhausted at the end of the meal and Dommie fell into a stuporous sleep almost instantly.

I did not want to leave Dommie's side but when Malissa handed me a plate of stew I remembered that I was starving. I sat at the small table, facing Dommie's bed, and ate like a field hand. Between bites I told Malissa and Henry of our predicament.

"Malissa, we have to do something about that harness." I sopped bread in the gravy left on my plate. "We have to widen it or make it longer . . . it won't fit me the way it is." Stuffing the wad of bread into my mouth, I added, "And can we pad my shoulders with something? I think we'll be picked up right away by another ship but what if we're not? We may have to wait for hours and there's no need to be uncomfortable."

82

We had not discussed the gold but Dommie certainly couldn't carry it and there were the same objections to Malissa or Henry carrying.

Henry turned to face the window as I unbuttoned my dress and dropped it to the floor. It was a matter of a few minutes for Malissa to lengthen the shoulder straps since they were made of leather belts tightened with an ordinary buckle. Leather thongs tied the straps, front and back, to a wider belt which hung loose around my hips. Thus, the bags of gold, when tied to this belt, would be concealed by the flare of my skirt.

One by one, Malissa very carefully tied each bag to the belt with the bag's leather drawstring. She alternated sides in an effort to balance the load but, even so, I felt the weight setting the straps into my flesh. I shifted uneasily, trying to move my shoulders to a more comfortable position. There wasn't one.

We became aware of noises in the passageway: feet clumping, loud male voices. As my heart jumped towards my throat, I looked at Malissa and saw her fear. She helped me wiggle into my dress, both of us fumbling with the front buttons.

"Ladies! Open the door!" It was no voice I knew. Malissa, unburdened, moved faster than I. With a backward glance at me, she opened the door.

I did not recognize the young soldier but Captain Hansen was standing behind him. He pushed the soldier aside and entered the room. I could tell from his expression that he did not approve of whatever it was he had come to say.

"The Lieutenant," he began in a loud, angry voice, "has ordered that you be sent ashore. You are to collect your belongings and be ready to disembark in fifteen minutes."

"We what?" I stammered, not believing his words.

The Captain's fists were clenched. "You have fifteen minutes to make ready. I've tried to intercede but we're casting off as soon as we have power and you are to be put ashore before that time."

"But it's almost dark. No ship will pick us up if they can't see us!" I was about to point out also that our trunks were stored somewhere in the bowels of the ship. How could I find and claim them in fifteen minutes? With the Captain's next words, however, I forgot the trunks.

"Ma'am, there will be no ships stopping here tonight or any other time. This place was once a wharf for loading goods, nothing more. There are no settlements for fifteen miles in either direction and no shelter that I know of. You're being set ashore to make your own way, however you can. I deplore this action but I'm a prisoner on my own ship and I have no say in the matter."

We were no longer the captain's responsibility, though it was clear he felt otherwise. What to do in the next few minutes was my only concern.

Stunned, I stammered, "There's nothing here but a wharf?" At his nod I continued, "No shelter of any kind?"

"No, ma'am, none that I know of. There is a road . . ." He shrugged.

Of what use was a road to us if we had no carriage, no horses? I was thinking fast. "Are we allowed to take a . . . a bed for my cousin . . . and bed clothing? We can't just dump her on the ground!

She's quite ill, Captain, as the Lieutenant well knows."

"You're certainly welcome to whatever you need for your cousin's comfort." He lowered his voice. "As soon as possible, I'll notify someone of your whereabouts. You could try signaling with a fire if you see a ship but I doubt if any responsible captain will stop." I thought he was out of words but he added, "I've packed a hamper of whatever I could find that you might use. There's some food, water, a knife, other things . . ."

The possible consequences of the lieutenant's order plus the weight of the gold was causing my knees to sag. I saw that Malissa had gone to Dommie's bed. Henry was a huge shadow against the papered wall. We seemed to be frozen, caught by a bright powder flash like photographic images on a silver plate. If we were to make the most of this situation I'd best get us moving.

With my sharp Yankee voice I said, "Thank you, Captain, for what help you've given us. And I do need men to carry my cousin's bed." I had no intention of allowing Henry out of my sight. He could have carried both beds without strain but, once alone on the wharf, would someone think Henry better off in the river and then put him there with a bullet? I could not take the chance. He must stay with me.

"Malissa, give Dommie a spoon of laudanum. No need for her to be upset by all this." Then I said to the captain, who had not moved, "Our two children are with the Ursuline Sisters in New Orleans. Antoinette and Elsas LeCompte. The Sisters have instructions and money in the event . . . in the event we are delayed. Will you see to this, Captain?"

"At the soonest, Miss O'Neal." He bowed.

I did not wait for the door to close behind him. "Malissa, help me wrap Dommie in this spread." We were gentle; Dommie slept.

"When it's time, Henry, you carry Dommie. And both of you stay close to me, understand?" I knew by Malissa's face that she understood only too well.

I looked around the room. There was nothing of value except for the laudanum and what was hidden in the bottom of my reticule. "We'll take my bag, Malissa, and both of us carry what bed clothing we can lift." Noise from the corridor and a fist pounding on our door told me that our escort had arrived.

At my nod, Henry bent to lift Dommie. He held her with such tenderness that I felt my eyes brim. Blinking furiously, I opened the door and motioned for the soldiers to enter.

CHAPTER X
August, 1862

In the waning light we watched the *Memphis Queen* move from the ancient dock and into the river current. A few of the soldiers waved as the huge wheel churned the ship away from the bank. From my seat on the mattress, I waved back. Why not?

Malissa and I watched until the ship disappeared around a curve. It was so quiet on the deserted river bank that I thought I could still hear the paddle beating water long after the ship was out of sight.

Malissa, standing with her arms crossed, looked down at me. "What now, Faith?"

I would have shrugged but movement tightened the straps, pained my shoulders. "I can't think of anything except to wait for Henry." Perhaps it had not been a good idea to send him to scout the area but I had to carry the gold until we found out if the towering trees were all there was nearby. It didn't make sense for me to be the one wandering in the woods. I wouldn't leave Dommie, anyway.

Malissa sat on the mattress next to me, her hand reaching to touch Dommie. "I'm thankful for the laudanum," she said. "It's kept her quiet."

"She seems better, I think. Don't you think so?" Just the fact that the soup had stayed down was reason to feel encouraged.

Malissa smiled at me. "Yes, Faith, I think so, too." I couldn't tell if she really thought so or if she was humoring me to keep up my spirits.

Still somewhat dazed, I looked around at the few goods we could call our own: the hamper, a mound of pillows and bed linen and the mattress with headboard and footboard but no support in between. The soldiers would have brought from the ship everything we asked for except that a blast from the ship's whistle had recalled them as they started down the gangplank with the first load.

It was the young guard from our door who had spoken. "I'm sorry, Ma'am, we can't carry no more. We have to go now."

I was about to object but knew that it would do no good. I took his hand. "Thank you," I said.

"I hope the lady gets well." He hesitated. "If I could stay, I would. You need a man to help."

I had smiled at his retreating back. I didn't particularly want his presence, I would rather have Henry, but I would have given a sack of gold for his rifle.

Dommie stirred and I turned in spite of the constraints of my harness. "I'm here, Dommie." Her temperature seemed normal and I took heart from this, too. "What is it, love?"

She opened her eyes. "Where the hell are we, Faith?"

Malissa and I both started laughing. Our Dommie was back with us again.

Dommie waited patiently for our outburst to end, her eyes falling shut. Wondering what, or how much, I should tell her, I decided that the truth was what she deserved to hear.

"We are on a mattress on the ground on the river bank," I said in a sing-song. "We have food, water, matches, bed-clothing, gold, a large knife, a small pot, cups and plates . . ." Out of breath, I stopped.

"Henry?" Her voice was slurred with tiredness.

"He's here, Dommie, we're all here with you." This seemed to satisfy her, for she sighed and her eyes closed again. I held her hand, rearranged her cover, smoothed her hair. I wanted to hold her in my arms, to lie at her side and hold her to me. "Malissa, help me out of this harness. We have to make some kind of shelter from the mosquitos."

Henry saved us from tent making by showing us the small three-sided shed he'd found not far from the wharf. He carried Dommie to the shed and held her, waiting patiently as Malissa and I followed, dragging the mattress. We put the mattress against the back wall and I waited with Dommie while they

89

went back to the wharf for the bed clothing, the hamper and the gold. Once Dommie appeared to be comfortably settled, I helped Henry cover the holes in the roof and in the sides with leafy branches which he'd torn from nearby trees. We draped the open side of the shed with sheets to keep out the hordes of mosquitos that bit through our clothing. Malissa's fire of dry branches gave off little smoke but that little bit helped discourage other flying insects.

We were fairly snug in our shed. Dommie drifted in and out of consciousness, restless. Probably the laudanum was wearing off. We thought it best not to give her more until we fed her. Malissa made tea and the three of us sat on the ground and sipped it, sweet and scalding, waiting for potatoes to boil. I mashed a tiny bit of boiled potato in a cup of hot water to make broth for Dommie and, while it cooled, Malissa, Henry and I ate our own potato soup.

"You feed Dominique while Henry and I go down to the river to get water for the dishes."

Malissa and I both knew perfectly well that the dishes could wait until morning when there'd be some light but I was grateful for the chance to be alone with Dommie. Henry added wood to the fire then held the sheet aside for Malissa, ducked under it himself, and they were gone into the darkness.

"Hold me." Dommie's voice was hushed, hardly loud enough to hear, but her eyes were partly open; I could see in them the reflection of the firelight.

"Oh, baby," I whispered to her, "oh, my baby!" I stretched out on the mattress by her side, covering both of us with the light quilt, then I took her in my arms. I felt her soft breathing as she leaned against me. We stayed like that, not moving, not talking. The only sound was the crackling of our small fire.

Finally I spoke, more to myself than to Dommie. "In the morning I'm going to find a horse or a boat or a carriage or . . . some way to get us out of here."

She stirred slightly. "No."

I knew why she objected. "I won't be gone long, love, just a little while. Only long enough to get help."

"Please." It was a pitiful plea, like that of a child who knows the adult is not going to listen.

"I'll never leave you, don't you know that? But I have to get help even if it means that I'm away for a few hours."

She shifted in my arms and I heard again, "No."

Why was I trying to reason with her? There was no way she could understand the seriousness of our plight or the fact that we had few choices in the matter.

She drew in a long breath. "If I rest for a while, I'll feel better. You'll see." This was quite a speech and I knew the effort it had taken.

Lightly, I touched her lips with my fingers. "Yes, you rest, baby, while I hold you." We were still together on the mattress when Malissa and Henry returned.

Henry added wood to the fire and Malissa reheated the broth. I sat cross-legged on the ground to feed Dommie, pleased that she swallowed most spoonfuls without gagging. To show that she was better she asked to feed herself but the spoon proved too heavy for her to lift.

"You just need rest," I told her, smiling because her eyes were open and she was looking at me and I knew she would live.

* * * * *

There was light in the sky when I woke. I sat up, stretching to relieve the stiffness caused by sleeping on the ground. Malissa had the fire going and a cup of tea ready for me.

"Do you want to eat before you leave?" she asked quietly. "We have bread and honey and preserves."

"I'll eat a little now. Is there any way I can carry water?" I, too, spoke in a hushed tone so as not to wake Dommie. She had slept almost through the night, awakening only when movement caused pain in her shoulders.

"We have a large jug of water and two bottles of wine. I'll empty one wine into a pot and fill the bottle with water." Malissa's face showed concern. "Do you have any idea how far you'll have to go?"

"No."

We were both silent as I ate, our eyes on the fire. I saw no reason to lie to Malissa. I didn't know how far I'd have to go or how long it would take, or if I'd find help in this wilderness. I didn't want to leave Dommie, but who was there to go if I didn't? I sighed. "Malissa, if I don't get right back . . ."

She shook her head. "You'll be back in time." She said this with such conviction that I merely nodded as I laced my shoes, wishing I had my sturdy, comfortable boots instead of these thin-soled fancy shoes that were inadequate for serious walking. Malissa handed me the bottle of water wrapped in my shawl and four gold coins from under the mattress. "Will this be enough?" she asked.

The coins shone dully in the light from the fire. Shafts of early sunlight came through holes in our shed roof and I moved my hand so as to catch the bright reflection on the gold. "Malissa, there's enough gold under that mattress to buy Mississippi, so if I . . ."

She stopped me again, touching my arm lightly. "You'll be back, Faith, and we'll be here waiting for you. Now go, before she wakes."

"I'll follow the road north, toward Memphis." I felt she already knew the direction. Vicksburg, the only city I knew of to the south of us, was too far. I was counting on finding a farming community or even a single family and I anticipated a walk of no more than three hours or so, then a fast ride back of perhaps an hour. "I should be back a little after noon, Malissa, if all goes well."

I pushed aside a corner of the sheet and stood for a moment in the opening of the shed. Henry was there. He handed me a tall walking stick, which he had cut and trimmed. "Thank you, Henry," I said, then added, unnecessarily, "Take care of them."

There was an overgrown wagon track which could have been called a road that closely followed the bank of the river. I walked through the dew-covered weeds, swinging the stick, my shawl slung over my shoulder and bouncing the contents against my hip with each step. As I walked, I found places to secret the gold, one coin to each hiding place under my gown and two coins in the shawl.

The track, barely visible, was dry earth with weeds growing tall in the middle and led under trees for the most part. Large oaks, swamp willows and other unidentifiable but shady giants kept most of the sun from my head and, had it not been for the urgency that propelled me, the walk itself would not have been unpleasant.

Not, that is, until I squished through mud as the track led down into a steaming morass of sharp-edged cane and slippery tree stumps, a place where the river had cut through its bank. The only way across was straight and, although the mud was soft only for a few inches of its depth, I stumbled and floundered and slid every step of the way, slapping mosquitos with one hand, holding my skirt high with the other.

I had no way to estimate my speed, but the sun, which had been peeping over the trees on the east bank when I started, was now a few degrees from directly overhead. I walked on through the dappled sunlight, seeing nothing but trees and occasionally the river itself, wondering at meeting no other travelers, seeing no other tracks, not even a trace that others had used the same route recently. I was unwilling to slow. I thought of Dommie constantly.

The August temperature, to which I had not become accustomed, was beginning to take its toll. I drank huge swallows from my bottle, stopping to do this only because I feared knocking out my teeth if I didn't. It did not bother me that I was alone, unarmed, the next thing to lost and almost fainting from the heat. It did bother me that my shoes, as they dried, were shrinking and cracking and that the blisters which had formed on my tender heels and toes had split open, bled and were now agonizing.

I simply could not walk farther. Almost in tears from frustration, I looked for a spot to sit.

The base of an oak provided a shady resting place. I leaned against its solid form and, eyes closed, pictured my feet with and without shoes. If I removed the shoes I did not think myself able to walk on bare feet more than a few steps over this rutted, littered trail. If I did not remove the shoes, even one step more would be impossible. Sighing, and with some difficulty, I removed the shoes. Blessed relief followed.

The sun told me that I had been walking three or four hours already. I upended my water bottle and drank all but a an inch or two of the precious liquid. Inspiration came as I swallowed the last drop. Of course! Tear my shawl into strips, fold the strips and tie them to my feet with smaller strips and I'd have instant moccasins. My idea was perfect but — more frustration — I could not tear the shawl; its fibers resisted every effort.

Determined to keep walking, I tore my more delicate undergarment instead. Though not my intention, this served a twofold purpose: my feet were somewhat protected and I could now continue walking cooler, for lack of a double layer of fabric flapping against my legs. With a measure of hope, I bound the useless shoes and almost empty bottle in the shawl, heaved myself upright and, cautiously at first but without undue pain, started again on my way.

The sun's rays, now directly overhead and blazing, were somewhat diverted by the canopy of leaves and I trudged northward, still following the wagon track which inevitably must lead to help for Dommie.

Was there a fate, foreordained, for all of us? Was my life following a prescripted path as I walked this one physically? What, I continued the thought, what if Dommie was going to get well no matter what I did? If so, I could just as well have stayed with her. Perhaps the Captain's lot was to turn the boat and come back for us. I pictured the *Memphis Queen* minus soldiers and the cozy cabin and Dommie in the cabin with me. Dommie, unclothed, waiting on the bed as I disrobed to join her on the clean-smelling sheets. Her sweet scent filled my head.

If there were any measures of self-determination, of free will, in this world then I would do whatever was necessary to be with Dommie. The thought of her smooth body was so exciting that I did not mind walking with bleeding, rag-covered feet through the clouds of mosquitos that my skirt disturbed.

Scrutinizing the ground directly ahead of my feet, my mind filled with cautious metaphysical meanderings, I almost failed to see the track that diverged from the one I was following. It was fainter, not as well defined, but it appeared to have been used recently by two horses. The riders had come in from the west, crossed over the track I followed and headed for the river bank. Then, retracing their steps, they had headed west again.

Heart pounding I stumbled in that direction.

The woods thinned as I walked away from the river and the trees gave only intermittent shade. Perspiration, dripping from my every pore, pasted my dress to my legs, making walking even more difficult. No matter! No matter at all.

Both hands on the walking stick as I plowed forward, I spoke aloud. "Dommie, love, I've found people! We're saved!"

CHAPTER XI
Thursday, August 28, 1862

The horse tracks led me away from the trees that crowded near the river and out onto a treeless, mushy plain filled with the same lethally-edged growth that I had encountered in the marsh. Looking somewhat like cornstalks, they towered over my head, growing close and thick like bamboo. As I pressed forward on rag-covered feet, the suffocating heat made me realize that the thin, blade-like leaves gave little protection from the sun. Each step caused a shower of tiny spears of silken fluff, like peach fuzz, not bad individually but causing great discomfort when landing by the thousands on my exposed flesh. No matter. The important thing was to keep going.

I do not know how long I thrashed my way forward before I realized that there were no horse tracks ahead or behind me, that the trail had disappeared. I had been blindly pushing my way through a forest of slashing green leaves, following nothing but my nose. I had to go back, find the trail again. I was in despair over the additional time this would take.

For the first few yards it was not hard to retrace my path; I had left a swath that a child could follow. After that, however, the stalks returned to their original stand, closing in as if I had never passed their way. Again, no matter. When I walked I left prints in the muck. Simply backtrack to find where my prints diverged.

Backtracking, however, was not the answer. I could not find my own tracks. I saw only wet clumps of roots, clinging to the steaming earth with tendrils as thick as my thumb. Wiping perspiration from my eyes, I bent to peer at what I could not see while standing — yellowish stems clutching the coarse black earth like curved talons. These may have been interesting botanically but were not helpful to my situation. Ah, well, there was always the sun as a guide.

I stared up at the sky, what I could see of it through the green spears, turning to orient myself to the sun's position. This movement shook a shower of fluff in my face. I closed my eyes to protect them and bursts of black spots appeared on the inner lids, swirling black spots dancing erratically in a haze of red. I planted my walking stick firmly in the loose earth and clasped it tightly, desperately hanging on with both hands.

It is debatable whether or not I could have fallen, the stalks were so close together, but upright or prone, one way or the other, I intended to keep going. I had already walked so many miles, surely a few more were within my reach. A minute until my balance steadied . . .

This, then, is how they found me; upright but with head bowed, clinging to a pole imbedded in the ground, talking to myself.

I heard a man's voice. "Lady! Is ye all right, lady?"

I looked up at the apparition towering over me. A horse? Surely, a horse! And something else . . . an appalling, hair-covered face! The hair moved, brown teeth appeared . . .

"Lady?"

I straightened, took a deep breath. "Yes, I'm all right. I'm just a little lost. Would you be so kind as to show me the way out of here?" I've found that politeness is always a good policy.

"Well, damn me! If ye ain't sumpthin'! Kin ye take my hand?"

I peered at gnarled fingers stretching down to me, the ancient hand matching the ancient face. I understood that he meant to pull me to the rump of his horse. "Yes, thank you, I can . . ." And I let him grasp my wrist and heave.

It was not until I was seated behind him that I saw another rider. I looked into bright blue eyes shaded by a floppy hat, a huge grin and curly, shoulder-length red hair. A girl, a young girl in faded pants and shirt, bareback on a mule. Her grin widened as I adjusted my skirt and tightened my grip on the shawl.

"We thought you were a pig. Come crashin' through grass just like one." She giggled. "Had my mouth set on pork, I did."

"I'm sorry to disappoint you." I grinned back to show that no offense had been taken at her joke.

The closeness of the tall grass made the horses uneasy; they snorted and back-stepped nervously. How pleasant it was to exit this place with my head high enough to breathe air instead of steam. I believe the animals took no more than a few steps and we were on firm ground, only a good stone's throw from three dilapidated wooden houses. Had I been four feet taller, I could have seen the roofs from the swamp.

My rescuer stopped next to the sagging, open porch of the center building and I let go of his waist, sliding from the horse's rump to the highest step. For some reason my knees would not hold me and I grabbed for one of the rough posts that supported the roof.

"Whoa, lady!" I heard a masculine voice and felt arms circle my waist, hold me from falling. "Set down here."

I collapsed awkwardly on the weathered planks of the top step. I heard the wine bottle slam to the floor as I settled myself, reminding me of water and how much I needed some. I reached behind me and began fumbling in the folds of the shawl, the bottle eluding my grasp.

"Can I help you, lady?" It was the girl.

"Yes, thank you, I'm trying to get my water bottle . . . in the shawl." I was trying to speak clearly but the swirling spots reappeared, distracting me, and I'm afraid that the only intelligible word may have been "water."

"Here, drink this."

Gratefully I reached for the tin dipper that appeared in front of me and upended it over my mouth, choking and spilling most of the cool liquid down my front. The water, both inside me and out, revived me. Another deep breath and the spots faded. "More, please."

I was circumspect with the next dipperful, sipping slowly, stopping between swallows to smile at the three-member audience watching me drink.

I handed the dipper back to the heavily bearded young man who, I learned, had been the one to save me from falling on my face. His name, he announced, was Hezzie and I was sitting on his steps.

"I'm Faith O'Neal." Then I nodded at the old man who was standing next to his horse. "I thank you, sir, for rescuing me." Seeing the bright smile on the girl's face, I added, "And thank you, too."

I waited for some seconds, then, seeing that they were also waiting for me to carry the conversation, I began, "I came here to ask for your help. I was a passenger on the *Memphis Queen* for New Orleans . . ." Some shift in their collective expression gave me pause. They looked from one to the other without turning their heads. Not a word passed between them but I could tell that some form of communication had taken place.

I broke the silence, carefully phrasing my next words in the unlikely event these people were Union sympathizers. "Federal soldiers took over the boat and put us ashore on a deserted wharf some miles south of here . . ." Again there was some furtive eye movement, passing through the three of them like wind ripples in a grain field. I hurried on, uneasy without knowing why. Using the young soldier's word for Dommie's illness, I said, "My cousin is gravely ill, near death from the flux and I have to get her to a doctor."

I looked from face to face, seeing no expression that I could identify. They were waiting, so I continued, "If you have a horse and wagon that I could borrow or rent and would tell me the nearest likely town . . ." I stopped. The two men were shaking their heads.

"No horse," the old man said, "No horse, no wagon." Hezzie nodded agreement.

"Do you mean that you don't have them to spare or that you don't have them at all?" I asked.

"Can't use no wagon and can't spare no horse.."

I think he was being friendly, just sparing of unnecessary words. I could appreciate that. "But you do have them?" I asked.

The three of them nodded in unison. The old man spoke, pointing to the horse he had been riding, "This here's th' horse we can't spare and the wagon's not got but three wheels."

My heart sank. "Isn't there a spare wheel somewhere that could be used? My cousin is lying on the ground, we have little food, almost no water except for the river and I've come so far . . ." I could not stop my eyes filling with tears. "Where am I to go for help?"

The old man's eyes narrowed as he looked at me. "Wasn't they others on that boat with ye? Where did they get to?"

To hide my sudden confusion I dabbed at my eyes with the shawl. The other passengers, all men I believe, had been put ashore yesterday morning. Presumably, they would also have headed towards Memphis but stumbled upon this place first, just as I had. I had not seen their tracks but they may have found a path easier than the blind trail through the swamp which I had followed. Where, indeed, had they got to?

I sniffed and dabbed at my eyes to give myself time to think. "I know nothing about the other passengers. They were put ashore . . . somewhere . . . they're probably in Memphis by now." I dismissed them by pointing to my rag-covered, muddy feet. "At least they had shoes and I, I'm walking on rags. Please," I implored, "can't you find it in your heart to help me . . . I can't let my cousin die!"

It was the girl who broke the silence. "I'll let you have my mule, I will."

Both men stared at the girl, then the old man spoke. "Hezzie, see can ye find a wheel."

Hezzie laughed. "Bet I remember where it's at, too."

"And, Hezzie, bring a pair of boots for Miss O'Neal after you've repaired the wagon."

I had not heard anyone walk on to the porch but the man's soft voice was coming from right behind me. I started to turn, to look up, but his hands pressed my shoulders, holding me in place. "Let me help you inside, Miss O'Neal, and I'll see what we can do for your feet." The hands moved down my arm to grip my elbows.

"I'll help, too." The girl bounced up the steps, took my forearms and pulled upward. I could have done my own standing if they had given me a moment to get my feet together under me; instead I was more dragged than not across the porch and into a tiny room crowded with a jumbled assortment of furniture. It was dim inside and, by the time my eyes adjusted, I had been pushed into an upholstered armchair, my feet lifted and a stool shoved under my heels.

The girl leaned elbows on the chair, her face almost touching mine. With a wave of her hand, she performed introductions, "This here's Lonnie and I'm Blest." As an afterthought she added, "My mule's Ho-ray-shus, same as th' hero." Then, without pause, "I can read, I can. Bet you didn't know I could read, did you?"

Before I had time to answer I heard that soft, melodious voice again: "Blest, we'll have time for that later. Right now we must see to Miss O'Neal's feet. Will you go outside and fetch a pail of water and some clean cloth and, Blest, wash your hands and face while you're about it. I can smell mule from across the room."

Blest skipped backward to the door, promising, "I'll read for you when I come back, I will."

The man knelt in front of me, his head bent, and took my right foot in his hands, untying and unwrapping the filthy rags. "Blest is a little impetuous at times but she has everyone's interest at heart." He put my foot back on the stool and lifted the left one, looking up at me as he did so.

I saw smooth, classic features, deep brown eyes and a clean-shaven face. His dark hair was slightly long and there was a sprinkle of grey at the temples. The room's windows were shuttered but in the light from the door I could see a spotless white shirt, an impeccable cravat with a diamond pin, a light-colored tailored suit. I know I stared but I couldn't help it. I had not seen such sartorial splendor since Europe.

His gaze moved slowly downward, stopping at my bosom. His expression, his intent was clear. This was not common rudeness; for a horrifying instant I thought he was going to touch me there.

"Blest is your daughter?" I stammered, my hand moving to pull together the open neck of my dress.

He smiled at me. "She belongs to all of us. We're a rather rough assemblage in this compound but Blest has charmed the worst of us with her generous heart. There is not a person here but would lay down their life for her."

He had finished unwrapping my left foot and now examined what he could see that wasn't covered with mud. "You are a brave young woman to have walked so far with your feet in this deplorable condition. Cleaning and some salve should help. That and some sturdy boots."

Before returning my foot to the stool he held my heel and lightly stroked my instep. Then his fingers began caressing my ankle. I jerked my foot from his grasp. We faced each other for a long moment. Then, smiling slightly, he stood and wiped his hands on an immaculate handkerchief that he drew from inside his coat.

I could not let him see my fear. "I appreciate your concern but, truly, I must get back to my cousin

as soon as I can. My feet . . . boots . . . could wait
. . . the wagon and the mule are . . ."

His fingers clasped my shoulder, pushing me back
against the chair. I looked at him in astonishment
and tried to pull away. He bent, his face much too
close to mine, that little half-smile on his lips.
"Certainly, I understand the urgency of your mission
but it will take some time to repair the wagon and
find a harness for Blest's mule. Won't you relax, Miss
O'Neal, and let us insure that you'll at least be able
to walk when you reach your cousin?"

His words were reasonable but his fingers gripped
painfully, and there was a tightness in his voice, an
undercurrent that made my heart pound. I gritted my
teeth and forced a smile. "Of course you're right."

He nodded and stepped away, and I closed my
eyes, feigning exhaustion although pretense was
actually unnecessary. I heard his steps move around
me, then a door open and close. My heart was racing
furiously. I had seen this man's likeness on Wanted
posters in Memphis. There was no mistaking those
smooth cheeks and deep-set eyes. These people were
the river pirates I had read about, so feared along the
river, so much in the news because they had robbed
the last Union payroll wagon, killed the driver and
two guards. They were murderers, rapists and who
knows what else, and I was smack in their midst and
completely at their mercy. These shacks must be a
facade. Their real camp, a fortified hide-away, was
probably located deeper in the swamp. And Lonnie,
with his stilted speech and courtly manner, was
reported to be their leader.

If I had kept my thoughts on where I placed my
feet instead of picturing myself in bed with Dommie,

I would not now be in this stupid, nay, perilous situation. I tried to think of escape but footsteps clattering on the porch claimed my attention.

Blest, spilling water and boots, tripped into the room. "I have boots for you, Lady, and water and cloths and the wheel's on and I'm coming part way." Breathless, she dumped boots and rags on the floor and banged the half-empty pail of water at my feet. "Lonnie says I can make up food fer you to take." She was excited at the prospect of going with me. Was Blest to be the way I'd get out alive? A dead Miss O'Neal wouldn't need food, would she?

"That's wonderful, Blest," I said, meaning every word, "I'll enjoy your company, dear."

"And she yours, Miss O'Neal." I had not heard him come into the room. He had an ointment jar in one hand. "Miss Lester will tend your feet then we'll try fitting boots that won't aggravate your injuries." He made an abrupt motion with his hand, pointing to the stool on which my feet rested.

A young woman, a lovely young woman, came from behind my chair and stood smiling nervously at me. I gaped at her nearly nude form, feeling my face burn as she sat on the edge of the stool and reached for my foot.

Until Dommie, I had not seen complete nakedness, even my own, and this woman was wearing what appeared to be naught but a man's shirt, even her feet were bare. Several buttons were missing and when she leaned to take my foot, her bosom was completely exposed. Had not her knees been pressed together, I would have clearly seen her private parts. She made a move to pull the shirt together but stopped when the man's hand roughly clamped her shoulder. I gulped and closed my eyes to hide my confusion and to hide from the sight of red welts and dark bruises on her legs and body.

"Du . . . du . . . Does this hurt?" she asked, gently sponging dirt from between my toes.

"No," I managed to choke. "No." My senses reeled at the unbelievable assortment of people gathered in this room and I was acutely embarrassed at the menial service, this much too personal service, the girl was rendering.

"What have you done with your shoes? Did you throw them in th' swamp?" Blest was hanging on the arm of the chair; her question gave me a clue to the disposition of some of their stolen goods. Were dead bodies also thrown into the swamp? Of course they were. Where else to lose them so effectively? What would happen to Dommie if my lifeless form were likewise hidden? No, this was unthinkable. Somehow, for Dommie, I had to stay alive.

"No, Blest, the shoes are still in my shawl. They'll not fit me now, would you like to have them?" I smiled at her, my little red-headed ticket to survival.

"Aw, I wear boots. Miz Lester'd maybe want them."

"Miss Lester has no need for shoes, Blest. She is adequately attired as she is." He cupped Miss Lester's chin possessively, forcing her head to turn so that she was looking up at him. "Aren't you, my dear?"

I saw fear in her eyes, quickly hidden. "Yes, I need nothing more than I have."

He moved his hand and I could see white marks where his fingers had pressed. The bastard! Clearly, this woman was a prisoner and one not likely allowed to ride out in a wagon. I knew there was nothing I could do to help her. My actions were geared to helping Dommie, nothing more. This young woman would have to find her own salvation.

My feet were now clean and dry, with salve covering the raw places, and I held them off the stool to be fitted. Blest had brought three pairs of boots, all only slightly worn, and I forced my feet into a pair made of soft black leather; they were small but I was past caring. Had they been taken from feet newly dead, or removed before death? I hoped the latter but the former was more likely.

"These seem to fit," I said as innocently as I could. "I think I'll be comfortable in them. How fortunate you had boots to spare." I gave Lonnie a grateful smile, hoping he would believe me too stupid to have suspicions of any kind.

"We's ready!" Hezzie's voice boomed into the room. There was a half-giggle lurking beneath his words, a kind of titter that I had not noticed when we were on the porch. He's simple, I thought.

Miss Lester stood, moving the stool, and I heaved myself awkwardly out of the chair. "Thank you for your help." I held out my hand which she took in hers.

"You're very welcome, mu . . . mu . . . miss." She squeezed my fingers then turned and walked through the door into the rear of the house. She did not look back.

"Is Blest to be allowed to travel partway with me?" I asked.

"I believe so, since she wants to go. She's taken a liking to you, Miss O'Neal, and she'll be safe with you." He patted Blest's hair fondly, looking down at her grin. "You may ride only as far as the river, Blest, then you must turn back. Miss O'Neal's mission is urgent and you wouldn't want to be the cause of a delay."

"No, not me!" She ran from the room and I watched her release the reins from the post and clamber into the wagon.

"Blest told me she had packed food, sir, for which I will be eternally grateful." I held out my hand. "My plan is to find a doctor for my cousin, then if . . . when . . . she recovers, take the next steamer to New Orleans to be with our family." It was good idea, perhaps, to have him believe that there was someone to miss us. "I will be happy to send back whatever amount you wish for the . . . rent of your wagon and Blest's mule."

"My dear Miss O'Neal," he interrupted, taking my hand in both of his, " I am happy to have been of service. There is so little here for Blest's amusement, anything that can give her pleasure is welcomed by all of us."

For a breathless moment I thought he was not going to release my hand. My legs shaking like trees in a storm, I managed to get past him and climb to the seat of the ancient wagon.

Blest was grinning from ear to ear. "Go, Ho-ray-shus," she shouted and slapped the reins on the mule's rump. Ho-ray-shus turned to give a loud snort then began moving his feet, too slowly for me but then I wasn't handling the lines. As we pulled out of the yard I looked back. Hezzie waved furiously; Lonnie and the old man lounged on the porch with two other, no . . . three other men, watching as we inched away. Where had the others been all this time? I had neither seen nor heard anyone else in the compound.

It was, perhaps, three o'clock. Even as slow as the mule was moving, we should be at the river in half an hour. Then Blest would leave me. The river would be the ideal place to dump my body and recover the mule and wagon, as I felt must be Lonnie's intention. It would not be reasonable to let me live, knowing his whereabouts as I did. Even if I had not recognized him today, chances are that I would see his face on a poster sooner or later and give his location to the authorities. I had only a short time to devise some way to keep the mule and wagon and save myself. Maybe speed was the answer.

CHAPTER XII
August, 1862

As we moved slowly away from the clearing, the mule's scrawny rump swayed with each plodding step. I listened absently to the thick sucking noise each hoof made as it was raised from the muddy trail. Our wheels echoed the sound as they squashed their way through the oozing muck that stopped at the hardpan which supported our weight.

Blest was chattering about everything and anything but I was only half listening. Since speed was obviously out of the question, I had to think of some other way to get free. But what? Could I hide in the swamp until night then make my way back to Dommie? Yes, maybe, but wouldn't they know that the wharf was my destination and get there before me? Even if I rode the mule? Of course they would. And what would they do to Dommie? I could not bear the thought. If only I had some way to fight back . . . a rifle, a sword, even a pointed stick.

Blest, hands loose on the reins, was waiting for me to speak, her bright eyes searching my face. None of this was her doing, I must not hold her at fault.

"I'm sorry, Blest, I didn't hear you. What did you ask me?"

"I asked if you wanted his gun since you had his boots? Lonnie wouldn't like it none but I think it's fair."

"What's fair, Blest? Whose gun?" At the word "gun" I became very attentive.

"This here gun, that's whose gun." She reached behind her and brought up the cloth sack that I thought contained food. "Here, I wanted you to have it since you have the boots, I did." She upended the sack in my lap and I caught the contents before they slid to the ground.

The pistol barrel gleamed in the afternoon sun, the pearl grips reflected a soft glow, and the cartridge belt, with all those lovely, shining rounds, gave off so bright a reflection that my eyes were blinded. I held the gun to my breast, I caressed its warmth, I was about to cover it with kisses but Blest interrupted.

"Can you shoot?"

I reached and squeezed her to me, the belt and gun hard between us. "Blest," I said, my chin resting on the top of her head, "honey, I can shoot the eye out of a snake at a hundred paces . . . from the back of a galloping horse, I can!" Perhaps a slight exaggeration about the distance, not the snake or the horse. I did not mention the thousands of rounds I had shot at anything that moved or stayed still. Spring through winter for most of my early years I had practiced under my father's watchful eyes until I could hit what I wanted.

Blest wiggled out of my embrace and gathered the reins in her two capable hands, her face red. "Then you're glad?" she asked.

"Yes, Blest, I'm very glad." I became calm now that I had salvation in my hands. Blest had given me the means to keep us alive. I gave silent thanks to the gun's previous owner, now undoubtedly rotting in the swamp.

"Would you take me with you?" Her voice was low and she was looking straight ahead, at Horatius. "I know the things they do aren't right and I want to get away." She lifted her floppy hat and wiped her forehead, pushing back damp red curls. She gave me a sideways glance. "Will you?"

"What do you mean, Blest? What things do they do?" I thought I knew but I wished confirmation.

"The men kill people. And Lonnie does, too. He's the worst one of all. He hurts Miss Lester, I hear her yell, I do . . . and the other ladies that was here before her. Lonnie takes ladies to the other men and they kill them when they get new ones. They'd be ready to kill you, too, but for me bein' here. That's why I gave you the gun . . . you can kill them first."

Although that was exactly what I planned to do, I started to shake my head. I was going to tell her that killing was wrong but she already knew that. I might have told her that I didn't kill people but she, in her youthful wisdom, already knew that I would. So I nodded instead. "Yes, I hope I can kill them before they kill me. But, Blest, I can't kill every one of them and if I took you with me they'd all be down on me at one time. You do see that, don't you? No matter how straight I can shoot, there're just too many of them."

Blest was nodding unhappily throughout all of this.

"And I have my cousin to take care of."

Blest interrupted, "I'd help, I would."

"No, dear, I simply can't take a chance. If you go back when we reach the river I can . . . take care . . . of whoever is sent to kill me and Lonnie won't know what happened. He may think the men have deserted."

"No, they never do that. He'd hunt for them and he'd kill them, he would."

"Well, at least the whole camp wouldn't come looking for me all at one time . . . probably only one or two would come to see what happened." I stopped abruptly. Was I actually sitting in a weather-worn wagon, drawn by an equally worn mule and discussing cold-blooded murder with a child? Planning the murder of several people, in fact?

"Blest, you do see that I'm right, don't you?"

"Yes, I guess. But Miss O'Neal, if I can leave some other time, will you take me in?" Her blue eyes were so earnest, her expression so hopeful that my heart went out to her. She was, after all, Dommie's savior, if I could keep control of the ambush I planned and if I could still shoot straight and if the bullets lasted, that is.

Gently, I took her chin in my hand, lifting her face so that she could see I meant what I said, "Blest, I promise to take you in whenever and wherever and you will always have my love." I leaned under the hat and kissed her damp cheek causing her face to turn the color of her hair.

"Where will I find you?" she mumbled.

"If I'm not killed we'll be in New Orleans. The Ursuline Nuns will know where I am." I strapped my beautiful revolver snug and low on my hip, enjoying the feel of it against my thigh.

"Blest, who will come for me, do you know?"

Her clear blue eyes, guileless, looked into mine. "Gran'pa and Hezzie." She thought for a moment then added, "Yep, it'll be them for sure. Lonnie thinks Hezzie needs practice." A shiver ran down my spine. Hezzie needs practice in murdering? Proficiency at rape? That this child could speak calmly of abominations that were against every law of God or man chilled me to the bone.

We had reached the river. "Go now, Blest."

She untied the horse and heaved herself into the saddle. "I'll see you in the city, I will." She turned the horse and, without another look, galloped back down the trail.

Relieved that she had gone without too much fuss and thankful that I could now make plans without interruption, I slapped Horatius smartly with the reins. "Move, mule," I yelled, slapping again. Horatius began moving and I found, with continuous encouragement of this kind, that he moved smartly.

I had never before planned murder. One part of me shrank in horror from the deed; another part hummed with joy at the knowledge that the deed could save my Dommie. But there was more to it than the deed itself. Somehow I had to do away with Hezzie and Gran'pa, or whoever was sent to kill us, get to the wharf and collect Dommie, Malissa and Henry, head north along the trail and get far past the road that I had followed to the camp. I would rather have murderers skulking behind me on this trail than readying an ambush ahead of me.

The sun was low; it would not be more than an hour or two before dusk. At least we had that in our favor. When the first men failed to return there would be some time of indecision before others were sent to find them. I hoped that Lonnie would think they were merely taking their time, making maximum use of us before assigning our bodies to the river. Whoever Lonnie sent would have to ride to the wharf, discover that there was no one there, then ride back to camp with the information and do whatever else they planned in the pitch-black dark. Good. We should have a fair start if all went well. And if I could kill before getting killed, that is.

Horatius moved at a good pace. We were well into the trees now and I began to look for a spot to hide the wagon. I found the perfect place for an ambush where the trail curved to the right, then curved again in the opposite direction. I walked Horatius and the wagon into the deep thicket along the river bank, tied the lines to a slender willow, then made my way back to the trail.

I could see my wagon tracks clearly. Walking carefully, because the boots aggravated my blisters, I found greenery that concealed me but gave full view of the trail. I squatted on the ground, my heart pumping from fear . . . and excitement and hope and dread. I took the gun out of the holster then replaced it. It was too soon. I must be calm, wait until I heard them coming.

Not five minutes passed before I heard horses. I recognized Hezzie's shrill laugh, heard the soft clop-clop coming nearer. They must have left the camp before Blest got there, passing her on the way out.

I drew the gun from the holster and stood, pressing back against a rough trunk, my eyes on the track, my heart pounding harder. In those few minutes, while waiting, I debated the method to use. Should I leap on the trail in front of them and give them a chance to shoot me? This was the honorable way, I suppose, to give them warning. Then, in my mind's eye, I saw Hezzie lying on Dommie's naked form, trousers around his ankles, his horrible hands on her soft breasts, his body thrusting between her legs . . . her head thrown back, neck straining as scream after scream filled the clearing.

The horses, with Hezzie and Gran'pa as Blest had predicted, moved past my oak. I stepped quietly out onto the track behind them, lifted the gun and pulled the trigger twice.

It had not occurred to me that I could profit from my deed other than by saving our lives. But, after I had dragged the bodies into the thicket by the river, I had two horses, two pistols, a rifle and a generous supply of ammunition as my reward.

The sun was behind the trees, the light fading fast, when I reached the little clearing. There was no one there. I jumped from the horse and ran to the shed . . . no one. All the walking and the killing hadn't helped at all. I should have stayed with her. I had left her and now she was gone. I sank to my knees in total despair, covered my face with my hands and let great sobs tear me apart.

"Foolish child, we're here." Malissa knelt at my side and turned me to face her.

I forced my mouth to speak. "Where's Dommie?" I blubbered. "Where is she?"

"We're down by the river." She pulled me, unresisting, to my feet. "She's fine, Faith . . . really!" Malissa led me through the tangled brush and I, not caring, lifted my skirt to wipe tears, exposing bare limbs to the world.

Malissa pulled aside leafy branches and we ducked into a naturally hollowed-out place in the river's bluff. In the dim light I saw Dommie. She was on the mattress, propped by pillows, and her arms were reaching for me.

Dommie sobbed, my arms tight around her slender shoulders. She felt so frail that tears filled my eyes again. Right there in front of Malissa I told Dommie that I would have died if anything had happened to her and she told me the same thing and we clung to each other, our cheeks pressed together. When, finally, I could bear to take my arms from around her, I wiped her tears with my fingers, searching her face, heartened by her smile. Someday I would tell her about Blest and Hezzie and the rest but now I had to get her away from here.

I stood to look at Malissa and saw Henry standing by her side. "Henry," I said, "we'll put the mattress in the wagon, you bring Dommie. We have to get out of here right now." I looked at Dommie. "Sweetheart, some people are chasing us and we have to move . . . fast!"

She stared up at me, then for the first time noticed the gun strapped to my side. Her eyes widened but she didn't say anything.

I looked down at her. "Don't be afraid, love." My smile was meant to reassure but I saw her sudden fear. I felt such sadness to see her thus . . . frightened, wanting to take some action, but without the strength to lift herself from the mattress.

She sank back on the pillows and closed her eyes, nodding wearily. My heart heavy, I motioned for Henry to lift her.

It did not take more than five minutes to get us on our way. Neither Malissa nor Henry commented when I handed each of them a gun. "Strap these on," I told them quietly. "We're probably going to do some shooting." I mounted Hezzie's horse, grateful to be off my hurting feet, and looked down at Dommie lying on the mattress. "Are you comfortable?"

"Now that you're back I am." She held her hand to me and I leaned to give her mine. "Faith, I can shoot. Do you have a gun for me?"

My brave darling. She couldn't even hold a spoon to feed herself last night. I looked into her green eyes and saw her love, her courage. "No," I said softly, "your job is to rest and get well." I turned away, overwhelmed by the thought of what I would have to do to her if I saw we could not get ourselves clear.

"Malissa." My voice was choked. "Slap that mule hard to get moving. Yell 'Ho-ray-sho' every once in a while, that'll do it."

Malissa nodded grimly and snapped the leather reins on the gray rump. With a lurch the mule and the wagon started moving. Dommie's eyes closed. I could tell that each jolt of the wheels was agony for her, but there was nothing I could do. I held my horse until Henry moved close.

"Henry," I said in a low tone, "ride next to me for now. I have to tell you what kind of trouble we're facing."

Henry brought his horse to my side and we waited for the wagon to get farther ahead so that Dommie couldn't hear.

"Henry," I started, "this morning I found a trail that led me to a pirate's camp."

CHAPTER XIII
August, 1862

We rode on, sunset over and the night sky beginning to settle into the blackness that allowed stars to shine through. The mosquitos were worse than anyone could imagine, their buzzing loud in our ears, their stings painful.

We had no way of telling time or of judging the distance we had covered. Our movement was slow but I had to make certain that, when we stopped we were far north of the trail to Lonnie's camp. I noticed the sky had clouded over and the wind from the west was much stronger; rain was not far off.

"Think we should get down by the river and sit out the rain, Henry?" I asked. "We should try to keep Dommie dry."

I caught up with the wagon and told Malissa what we wanted to do. Dommie, exhausted, had fallen asleep, looking like a lump on the mattress, so completely covered for protection against the hordes of biting insects.

Malissa said softly, "Whoa, Horatius . . . whoa." The mule stopped and a second later Dommie sat up with a frightened cry, fighting release from the covers.

I slid from the horse into the wagon bed and soothed her, helping unwind sheets as I did so. I knew my boots were filthy and had no place on her bed but I wanted to touch her, to reassure her.

"We're going to rest for a while, Dommie. It's going to rain and we need to cover you." She nodded, her hands clinging to mine.

The wind had picked up force. We heard tree limbs slapping against each other and little spatters of rain began just as we made our way off the trail on the river side and into a willow thicket. It was hard to see but if we couldn't, neither could anyone else. We had no way of knowing if we were adequately concealed so Henry tied his horse with us, took the rifle and walked back to the track to act as sentry.

Dommie, unable to stand alone, clung to the wagon's side, Malissa's arms holding her upright while I slid the mattress to the ground and wrestled it under the wagon. Then Malissa and I helped

Dommie get settled. We leaned leafy branches against the wagon's sides and a quilt over Dommie for what protection it could offer from insects and rain. There wasn't anything we could do about the water which was sure to drip through cracks in the wagon bed.

After Dommie was snug, I walked towards the water's edge to relieve myself and tripped over a thick rope tied around a tree and leading to the water. Curious, I inched my hands along the rope until I found the other end tied to a kind of floating deck.

My heart almost stopped. Of course! River pirates had to have something that floated. How else could they get out to a passing barge in order to pirate it? Finding this meant that we were probably very close to the trail that led to the camp. Pirates wouldn't hide their water transportation miles from their place of operation, would they? No, they would have to be close so as to have quick access.

I scrambled through the thicket. "Malissa! Malissa! Find Henry . . . we have to get out of here!"

I could tell that the constant jostling of the wagon caused Dommie great discomfort; Malissa and I heard her helpless moans whenever the wheels crashed into a hole. I thought of holding her on the saddle in front of me. I thought of Henry holding her; his great bulk could cushion her, his huge arms protect her from much of the horse's uneven movement. I thought of the men sure to be searching behind us and weighed Dommie's immediate discomfort against our chance of getting away. I looked at Dommie, curled in a little ball on the mattress, not sleeping, not even resting but not in our way, either, if we should need to ride fast or shoot faster.

"Malissa," I urged, "get that mule moving."

Hours later, all of us soaking wet, we pulled off into another thicket. It was still drizzling but I began to see breaks in the clouds and a sliver of moon brightened the sky occasionally. Twice we had made use of Henry's great strength to lift the wagon from a hole when the mule alone could not. It was a relief to all of us to stand still, even in the rain. We made Dommie as comfortable as we could under the wagon and the three of us hunched on the wet ground nearby. My nerves were so shaken that rest, as much as I needed it, was impossible. My thoughts kept gnawing at the things I should have done.

"I have a mind to go back and try to untie that flatboat," I told Henry and Malissa. "I don't know why I didn't think of it right then."

"You told me it was resting half up on the bank," Malissa said. " Anyway, it might not have been theirs, have you thought of that? And how could you have freed it? Are you that strong?"

"No, but Henry and I could have tried. And it was theirs, I'm sure of it! How many lives would be saved if they didn't have their raft? Dozens maybe." I slapped a mosquito and another instantly took its place.

Malissa touched my arm. "Faith, right now saving four lives positively is better than dozens maybe. Let it be." Henry nodded agreement.

I yawned and stretched. "We should get going."

"We haven't been here ten minutes! Let the animals rest even if you won't."

I itched, my boots were full of water, my feet throbbed painfully and my clothes were stuck to me. I had not eaten since who knows when and I was tired

125

. . . tired of walking and tired of riding, tired of being tired.

Malissa moved closer and pulled me down so that my head was in her lap. "Henry, get a sheet, please, so we can keep some of the mosquitos off." I started to protest but Malissa held me there, patting my back soothingly. "Rest, child, we'll take care of your Dommie."

I fell asleep instantly, worried mind, mosquitos and all.

* * * * *

Some hours later the night sky was clear and bright with moonlight. Horatius was moving at a good clip and Dommie, awake, was leaning on pillows propped against the wagon's side, sleepy eyes watching me.

I pondered the change that had taken place among the three of us. During my weeks in Dommie's home and from what I saw of her, Malissa had seemed strong and mysterious, almost all-knowing, and I had been somewhat in awe of her. Her attitude towards me had been . . . not friendly but not unfriendly either. She had Dommie's confidence and, more than that, Dommie often deferred to her. But that afternoon on the boat, Malissa had seemed to give Dommie into my care. Had it been only that my color gave me an authority that Malissa did not have?

"Are you tired, Dommie?" I asked. "Would you like to sleep now?"

"I think so." She smiled up at me, the moonlight bright on her face. "Are we going to ride all night? You must be tired, too."

126

Her voice seemed stronger and I took heart from that. I had told her only that we were being chased and it was a measure of her faith in me that she accepted my judgment without asking who or what . . . or why. "I think we're all doing fine, right Malissa?"

"At least the wind has blown some of the mosquitos away. I'm thankful for that. And, yes, I'm fine. We can keep going as long as this mule can find the trail."

The mattress was squishy from rain but at least it helped cushion some of the jolts. Dommie curled up and pulled the sheet back over her head. I hoped she could sleep but the wagon wheels seemed to seek out every hole in the path.

It had been a long day and the night seemed even longer. I asked myself, am I really riding for my life? Have I, today, actually killed two men by shooting them in the back? My thoughts were incoherent. I shook my head to clear it, straightened in the saddle, and turned to ride back with Henry.

Henry began to drop back and I followed his lead until the wagon was well out of sight ahead of us. "Henry, I feel it too," I whispered. "They're near, aren't they?"

Henry nodded and held up his hand, palm facing me. We both stopped. At first there was nothing, just frogs screaming at the moon and night birds calling raucously, wheeling over the trees. Then another sound. Horses . . . horses moving at a trot . . . several horses!

We dismounted. I moved to the right side of the trail and Henry disappeared into the brush on the left. My horse, tired, stood quiet while I tied his reins to a bush. Unconsciously, I wiped my hands on my skirt. Was it to dry them or to wipe away the sin?

The sounds grew louder.

What, I thought, what if these were innocent people? They could be travelers, coming from Vicksburg; they could be soldiers assigned to duty in Memphis. Was I to kill again without knowing who was to die? I sighed in despair, knowing we couldn't stop the riders to ask their identity, knowing we must shoot before they had a chance to.

I could hear the squeak of leather and the rough breath of a snorting horse.

I shot first at the rider on my side of the road, then at the rider in the middle. I heard another shot as I got off my second one. The horses, frightened, created a jumble as they reared and tried to outrun their fear. One rider, his heel caught, was dragged back down the road and out of sight. The other two lay where they had fallen.

Cautiously I approached the still forms. Outlined in the center of one shirt was a small, irregular, blackish shape; it appeared wet in the shadowed light. Half-opened eyes, unmoving, stared at the sky. Clenching my gun, holding my breath, I moved to the one lying face down. My fingers relaxed when I saw the wound the bullet had made in exiting his back and I let out a great gulp of air. This one would not stir again, either.

"We have to find the other one, Henry. He may not be dead." I had little doubt that he was but I had to make sure.

We did not have to look far. The horse had stopped and now grazed uneasily in the middle of the trail, his rider still hanging by a leg. We approached slowly, alert to any movement. When I saw the bloody chest and the rivulets of dark liquid that had bubbled out and dripped to the ground, I knew the man breathed no more. I leaned over and peered at him. His moonlit face was one I remembered from Hezzie's porch.

I holstered my gun and began laughing. I could not stop, my shoulders shivering as I fought to hold back tears. Henry put his arm around my shoulders and gently turned me away from the body sprawled on the ground, guiding my stumbling feet carefully around the other two silent forms. He lifted me to my saddle and walked my horse back to the wagon.

I slid off my horse, thudded into the wagon and crawled into Dommie's waiting arms.

Malissa came to the wagon and reached to touch me. "I have never known anyone as brave as you, Faith. You've saved our lives twice today. We can never repay you . . ."

I started sniffling. Dommie held me. "Hush, love. Please don't cry." She patted and soothed and I began to feel better. All except my feet, that is. Walking even that short distance had rubbed new raw spots and my feet were too painful to bear.

I tried to slide off the wagon but Malissa stopped me. "Henry and I can take care of those other things but someone has to stay with Dominique."

Put that way, I could hardly object. I pushed myself to the front of the wagon bed and backed into Dommie's waiting arms. She rested her chin on my shoulder, her arms around mine, her cheek against my hair. I relaxed and leaned into her. Her lips brushed my ear, her arms tightened as she whispered soft words meant to soothe and comfort me. If I closed my eyes, I could imagine, nay, almost feel her doing more. Why is it, I asked myself, that I feel so . . . so receptive. This isn't the time or place for lovemaking. I wished my body knew that. But my body didn't know it so I sat in the circle of Dommie's arms, ignoring desire that stabbed at me like a thousand needles.

* * * * *

We now had more horses than we knew what to do with but we couldn't leave them for Lonnie to collect. Henry tied them in a string behind the wagon, piling the rifles, shells and gun belts in the wagon and near dawn, we started towards Memphis again.

Before the sun was up, we rode through thick tendrils of fog that lay close to the ground; then, as the sun climbed, the mushy trail began to heat and the horses' feet disappeared in steam. As we moved, we ate breakfast of hard bread dripping with honey and washed down with wine. Dommie sat up, leaned against the wagon's side and nibbled a little. Her shoulders were stiff and too much movement was painful but the wounds were dry and there didn't seem to be any infection.

We traveled slowly, at little more than a walk, because the track was overgrown in some places and washed out in others, causing us to detour often. Dommie made the best of her bouncing bed, even sitting up for short periods. We rode along high bluffs and through leafy forests following the course of the river. Sometimes we were so close that we could hear swirls sucking at the bank and see trees as big as houses bobbing in the current.

From our high vantage point we began to see cultivated fields off to our left but no way to get off the bluff and down to them. "I'm going to look for another road. It doesn't make any sense at all that there's only this . . . this misused wagon track. There must be something better!" I turned and called, "Henry, come ride up here for a while, I'm going exploring."

I picked the easiest way down the incline that sloped from the bluff and walked the horse carefully through a marsh like the one that had trapped me yesterday . . . was it only yesterday? Once on solid ground, I went straight west and almost immediately found what I sought: a road, a well-traveled road. We had not seen it from the bluffs because of the trees. I rode north on it for not more than a half mile to find a narrow lane that intersected. This one led past a small kitchen garden to a house, I could see the slanted roof through the trees.

Cautiously, pulling at my skirt to cover as much of my legs as possible and keeping to the center of the track, I rode toward the weatherworn structure. There was, after all, a war in progress and strangers, even a barefoot woman, loose hair trailing, boots dangling from her saddle horn and astraddle a horse, could be suspect — especially one with a pearl-handled Remington strapped low on her hip and a Henry repeating carbine in the saddle holster.

Five pairs of eyes watched as I rode towards the porch. Keeping my hands in view on the saddlehorn, I greeted the family group. Mother, father and three children were friendly, curious, and, I learned, not very knowledgeable about the war. They knew about the Federal Army capturing Memphis in June and about the troops who now secured the town; last summer they had heard of Bull Run from a passing tinker but Shiloh, notwithstanding its closeness, was just another word and the river battle for New Orleans might as well have happened on a distant star.

"I don't aim to get into any fighting," the man said adamantly. "It's hard enough digging a living out of this ground. I ain't got time to shoot at no Federals 'less they get bothersome. Live and let live." He often saw blue uniforms on the road but they had not disturbed him or his crop. He and his family were isolated, close to, but out of the political turmoil. They were Southerners, yes, but uninterested in the Confederacy's claim to sovereignty, probably not even sure what the word meant.

I asked for food I could buy with gold, some water, and had some men come around looking for a wagon and a mule and two ladies?

Assured that yesterday and today they had seen no one traveling in either direction, at least during daylight, I hoisted my crock of food and a covered tin of water and almost rode away without asking how far to Memphis. I explained that we had been on the old road following the turns of the river, because we had not known about the good one that ran in front of his place.

The farmer, anxious to do his best by me, lifted his sweat-stained hat and scratched thinning hair. "Memphis is," he declared decisively, "not more than a day by mule and wagon." If we had stayed where we were, on the old track that followed the bluffs, we

132

would not have reached Memphis or any other place during this century; so much did it wind with the turns of the river.

Armed with this knowledge and the food and water, I rode back to the bluffs overlooking the river.

Malissa had decided to make camp. The horses were stubbed nearby and a crackling fire was waiting to heat thick slices of smoked ham, string beans, squash and onions stewed in their own savory juice and the golden corn cakes I had in my bundle. We mixed wine with Dommie's water, to help build her strength, and grinned happily when she insisted on sitting with us and feeding herself the little that she actually ate.

We seemed to be a carefree bunch, enjoying a summer picnic on the shady river bank. My carbine, however, was propped in easy reach. Malissa, Henry and I wore revolvers and, to please Dommie, from our store of armaments we placed a shiny new, fully loaded, Lefaucheux on the blanket next to her. I knew beyond any doubt that we were hunted with a ferocity that would escalate when three more of the hunters failed to return.

I told them that the good, well-traveled road wasn't as shady as the bluff. "So it's too hot for Dommie to travel right now. The other road is much smoother but we'll rest here until the sun is lower."

Malissa, sitting on the blanket next to Dommie, had been chewing on her thumbnail. "When we leave here you'll have to wear the gold again, Faith. We can't chance leaving it under the mattress anymore, not on a public road. Also —"

"I'll carry some," Dommie offered.

"No!" Malissa and I chorused. Then we had to laugh at Dommie's thunderous frown.

Malissa, still smiling at Dommie, continued, "It occurs to me that they'll be searching both roads. They knew you'd head north, Faith, and they wouldn't take a chance on missing you."

"So," Dommie mused, "the others are more likely behind us . . . after last night." Her eyebrows raised slightly, she searched our faces and found confirmation. "And we have no way of knowing when they'll turn up or how many."

We sat silent for a moment then Dommie said, "My being in that wagon is what's holding us back!"

I started to protest.

Dommie smiled slightly and took my hand. "No. We could move faster if I was on a horse, too." She squeezed my fingers. "I'm so damn tired of that wagon! Please, let me ride."

The Dommie of a few days ago would have simply told us to bring her one of the horses. Never would she have asked my permission to ride.

There was color in her cheeks, her eyes were bright and she knew I would say yes.

CHAPTER XIV
August, 1862

Horatius was left in the farmer's care. Henry and I pushed the wagon off the bluff and into the river.

We waited until dusk to begin our journey. The extra horse was tied behind Malissa, the gold was harnessed to me and, except for Dommie, we each had a rifle at hand.

Dommie needed help in mounting but, once in the saddle with a sheet under her and one covering her lap because of the constraints of my nightgown, she seemed strong enough. She insisted that we push ahead immediately.

"Wait," I said and offered to bind her feet.

"Oh, no. If you can ride with bare feet, so can I." She wheeled her mount and galloped away at full speed, leaving me open-mouthed and causing the three of us to string out behind in order to catch up.

I reached her first, our horses crashing together as I raced alongside. Fright made me want to shake her. I leaned, grabbing for her reins, but she twisted away and I caught her sleeve instead.

"Are you out of your mind? Stop this horse!" I pulled her arm. "They could be waiting and you'd race right into them!"

Eyes wild, she slashed with her reins, hitting my arm, my shoulder, narrowly missing my face. She was screaming, "Let go! Damn you! Let go!"

I released her, pulling back, leaning away from the whip-like straps, raising my arm to protect my face. The leather whistled through the air again and again. Dommie's voice was venomous. "Don't touch me . . . don't ever touch me!"

She rammed her horse into mine, savagely beating at me as I tried to get out of range. Behind us I heard Malissa shouting. Then Henry came between Dommie and me and I moved my horse away from both of them.

The night had suddenly become icy cold and I shivered. I was thankful for a well-trained horse. A touch to the reins faced him north and the pressure of my heels set his feet moving. Behind me, and becoming less distinct as I moved away, I heard Malissa's murmured questions and Dommie's sobbing replies but I could not make out words. Just as well, there was nothing I wanted to hear.

"Faith?"

I knew I was totally alone, so where did the voice come from?

"Faith, please."

Instead of the clippety-clop of one horse, I now heard the sounds of two. I was intrigued by the soft music that an iron shoe makes on dried river sand. Without trying, I had filled my mind with the gentle rhythm, my body swaying in time with the clip-clop, clip-clop.

"Are you hurt, Faith? She didn't mean to hurt you."

I turned my head to look at the person riding next to me. "No, Malissa," I said calmly, politely. "I'm not hurt. Just a little sting here and there."

Malissa's voice was choked. "Faith, she's tired and frightened and ill and she just lashed out . . . she didn't mean . . ." and here her voice faded then picked up again, "Please, you have to believe me. She always dashes off that way, like a . . . a crazy person. She knows what she did was stupid and you were right to stop her. Faith?" Now her tone softened, "Faith, you know how we feel about you, don't you?

No, I only knew that I was alone again. And I was tired and frightened, too. My mind signaled my mouth to move, "Malissa, you don't have to apologize for Dominique. I know my place now. Let's just try to get on down the road like we planned, as best we can." I hesitated for a second, then added, "You might ask her to please stay back with the rest of us, if you will."

* * * * *

We settled into a pattern. I rode ahead, Henry followed in the rear, Malissa and Dominique close together in the middle. Several times during those first terrible hours Dominique called my name and I heard how choked with tears she was but I wasn't going to answer so I rode on, silent, looking straight ahead.

My heart was so heavy that I wondered why I didn't die. I wanted to. She had meant so much to me, how could I mean so little to her? I had not changed in my own eyes. Why had I changed in hers? When had I become a person who had no right to chastise her for behavior that threatened her safety? When had I become a person to be cursed and whipped for trying to protect her?

I didn't want to think about the words she had whispered to me or how her hands and her mouth felt on my body those many times we had made love . . . so, of course, my mind kept flashing these images over and over until her soft whispers were a scream in my head.

I should force myself to concentrate, to make some kind of plan for the empty, senseless years ahead. I wasn't that much different from before. Except for murdering five men, I was still the same person. Except for having loved Dominique, except for still wanting her beyond all reason, I was the same. But she was who she was. Perhaps I was well out of it. The world is big, I thought, somewhere there's a place for me.

I glanced behind then signaled for us to stop. Dominique was slumped, swaying in the saddle,

Malissa's hand outstretched, steadying her. "We'll rest," I said and walked my horse off the road.

Dominique and Malissa talked in low tones for a minute then Malissa called out to me, "Faith, we can rest later, please let's keep going!"

I started to object then I shrugged, remembering that it wasn't my place to protect Dominique from herself. I did not want to risk another beating. We rode on.

Either the farmer's estimate was wrong or we had ridden faster than it seemed because we reached the settlement on the west bank of the river, across from Memphis proper, before sunrise. We had to wait for the ferry to take us across, so we tied our weary horses in front of the Gayoso Hotel as the sun came from behind dark, glowering clouds.

Henry had to help Dominique dismount. She almost fell into his arms. Malissa and Henry supporting her, we proceeded across the walk and through the ornate glass doors. I was glad that it was early and that we were unobserved as we waited for the clerk to appear.

I was given a room on the second floor and, without speaking, I turned from the desk, climbing the stairs with some difficulty, the gold having gained weight since last night. Before I turned from the stairs into my corridor, I leaned and called down, "Don't forget my bath water." Crude of me, perhaps, but I was beyond all caring.

* * * * *

I sat by the tall window to examine my filthy, hurting feet. Inside me was a numbness that made it hard to concentrate. I looked at the raw places on my right foot and, before I put my foot to the floor, forgot what I had seen. Over and over I heard Dominique's voice: "Damn you . . . damn you." I saw the loathing on her face, felt the leather stinging my flesh.

I hefted my left foot to my knee and touched at the hurting places. Dominique's image came between me and my foot, her voice hateful: "Don't touch me . . . don't you touch me!" I sighed and stared out the window. Thank goodness I had managed to hang on to my jewelry. Idly I wondered how much I could get for it, remembering the fortune in gold to which I had no claim. Would the hotel take gems in settlement of my account? I would have to ask.

I heard knocking and, wincing, I hobbled to the door to admit the bath attendants. They agreed to look in their closets for shoes and something suitable that would fit me until I could find the service of a dressmaker. "The war," I said. They smiled, happy to help.

Bucket after bucket of steaming water filled the tub and, after they left, I sank into it slowly but gratefully; then I just sat, numb, staring at the window. I had nothing to wear except filthy rags so after I scrubbed I heaved myself out of the tub, dried, folded the bath towel around me and dozed in the chair until the maids returned.

"Will these do?" the youngest one asked, holding for my inspection a serviceable gown, voluminous underclothing, hose, and a pair of sturdy shoes.

"We'll see." Wearily I dropped my towel and reached for the undergarments, smiling to myself as the maids twittered and turned away. At least, I thought, I'm not so modest anymore.

Finally dressed, I used the comb from my bag, made sure the gold was pushed far under the mattress, and carefully locked the door behind me as I left.

The desk clerk, more curious than a cat, informed me in a conspiratorial whisper, "The military police are located a few squares west of here, but I can provide hotel transportation to their office if you'd rather?" He wanted to know why I needed police but couldn't bring himself to ask outright.

"I'd rather," I said, and soon found myself seated across from a Major Claypoole and two aides, all attached to the office of the military commander of Memphis, the Army of the Mississippi. They were most interested in what I had to say.

I began at the beginning and at some point the Major had me repeat this or that part of my story, dwelling particularly on the location of the pirate camp, the incidents aboard the *Memphis Queen* and the means we had taken to protect ourselves.

I told them what I could recall, then I added, "The horses and the weapons we took from the bodies are in the hotel stable. Mrs. LeCompte, her maid and manservant are at the hotel, also, and will be happy to confirm or clarify any details."

I sipped the water provided for me and then, my mouth still dry, said what I knew had to be said without prompting from these Federal officers. "I, personally, killed the first two men and, as I've told you, I also shot and killed two of the other three who were after us." My throat seemed to be closing so I sipped again. "If there's to be a penalty for . . .

for murdering these men, I'm the only one to pay it. Henry simply did as I instructed, and Mrs. LeCompte and her maid had no part in the deaths, I assure you."

Major Claypoole cleared his throat. "My dear Miss O'Neal . . . far from a penalty, you deserve a medal! There're a number of rewards for information concerning these men and I believe the amount is considerable. The man called Lonnie . . . did you hear any other name for him?"

Noon came and went but I wasn't in the least hungry. I had walked out of the hotel without waiting for breakfast and I should have been ravenous but my relief at finding myself free from death by hanging was palpable. Reiterating my belief that the camp's actual location was deeper in the swamp, I added other details as they came to me, speaking bitterly of Lieutenant Barker.

Finally they had heard enough. "Based on your information, Miss O'Neal, we should be able to clear out this nest of vipers." The Major came around the desk and patted my arm; he must have seen my fear. "Don't you worry about reprisals. They'll all hang, I assure you."

"Can you tell me why Lieutenant Barker had to take our boat in the first place? Why he'd put helpless women ashore?" No one smiled at my use of the word helpless.

The Major actually looked embarrassed. "There is no Lieutenant Barker attached to this command, Miss O'Neal, so I can't speak for his actions. I'll have this looked into. I can only say that he must have misread the orders concerning contraband. He'll be properly reprimanded."

142

"I need rest, Major, so if we're finished . . ." It took an effort of will to lift myself from the chair.

The Major led me to a carriage. "I don't think it will be necessary to bother Mrs. LeCompte at this time. Your information should be sufficient." He took my hand in his and spoke warmly, his feelings genuine, "You have done us a great service, Miss O'Neal. These men are responsible for the deaths of three of my men, and they have defied all of our efforts to locate their headquarters."

I settled myself on the carriage seat, "Will you let me know when they're captured?" Then a thought occurred to me, "No one has to know that I'm the one who . . ."

"No, my dear, no one will know."

Satisfied, I withdrew my hand from his then leaned my head on the seat and closed my eyes.

I was exhausted. Hunger may have played a part but what I needed most was sleep — hours, days of sleep. I also had to think about a future, but that could wait until tomorrow when I had better control of my feelings.

The hotel lobby seemed crowded but I was too tired to be curious. The clerk had my key ready; his hand reached across the counter to meet mine so that I did not stop but took the key while hobbling to the stairs. Increasingly, I needed the bannister's support to help me ascend and with each step I heard, behind me, the rising volume of excited voices. Maybe the war's over? Whatever the occasion, I would deal with it after I'd rested.

CHAPTER XV
August, 1862

Rest was long in coming; tears came first.

After tears, sleep.

With sleep, dreams.

Dominique, her long hair flowing in the river's current, was reaching for me but I was caught by live green tendrils that held me immobile on the river bank. My limbs encircled, I could move only my eyes. She called my name. I cried out and tugged at the vines but they were too strong and the river too swift. Dominique's slender arms, white in the brown water, disappeared and I was alone. Despair as deep as the river claimed me. My cries echoed from bank to bank but Dominique could not hear. I sobbed . . .

. . . And jerked awake. I wiped my eyes and found my face wet with tears.

"Will you ever forgive me?"

Was I still dreaming? My body stilled so that I could listen for that soft voice again.

I heard a deep sigh, like a muted sob, and I turned my head in the direction of the sound. Dominique sat in the window chair, her white gown ghostlike, her ebony hair falling like a dark blanket on her breast. It was too dark to see her features clearly and she sat as still as stone.

"What?" I stumbled over the word, sitting up on the side of the bed. My dream still so real that I thought I should hear water dripping from her.

"I know I hurt you deeply but . . . I beg you to forgive me!"

My mind whirled, despair still fathoms deep. I wondered if to forgive meant also to forget, for I could not forget. Her betrayal burned like a new brand, blistering under the glowing iron. Removing the iron could not erase the mark. I could cover it with forgiveness but it would remain, indented, a scar, irreversible.

"Please, Faith, won't you answer me?"

How long had I been staring? She would sit there until I gave her some kind of answer and I couldn't bear her nearness. I must speak.

"I . . . I can't."

"You can't answer, love?"

"No, I can't for . . . forget." I meant to say forgive. I can't forgive. But she called me love.

She whispered now, "I won't forget either. I watched you turn away from me and my life ended at that moment. I would give all I have in this world to erase what I did. I had no right . . ."

"I loved you."

At that she hunched in the chair; her sob tore at my heart.

Ah, no! My tongue had tripped again! I intended to say "I love you," meaning that I loved her now and I would love her forever, but it had come out in the past tense. Did this mean that I once loved her but did no more? My feelings were such a jumble that I didn't know, myself, what I meant.

"Dominique?" She could not answer. "Dominique!" I needed sleep and we weren't going to get anywhere with all this. She should go.

I knelt in front of her and took her hands in mine. In the faint light from the window I looked at her face; it was ravaged by tears, drained by illness, bereft of hope.

She looked into my eyes and her hands, those soft, loving hands, crept around my neck and pulled me closer. Our lips met, salty, wet with her tears; we kissed. "I love you," she said into my mouth. "Oh, how I love you."

I rose and guided her from the chair. She sat on the bed, hands in her lap, face turned to mine, waiting for me to lead. Gently, I helped her lie back on the pillows, then stood silent and looked down at her outline against the patterned coverlet, at her slim length, her face white, framed by the blackness of her hair. She reached for me but I moved away.

I had fallen, exhausted and fully dressed, on the bed this afternoon. I still wore what I had on then. While Dominique watched, I removed my outer garment. Then I sat on the bed next to her and gently touched her cheek, feeling the wetness of tears. Her arms reached but I held back, shaking my head, moving my hands to cover her breasts, searching with my fingers for the hardness that appeared as I touched. I caressed the soft mounds, lightly circling the raised centers, erect and hard under the fabric of her gown. Now I took her breasts in my cupped hands, squeezing gently, releasing pressure to squeeze again. I could have been kneading dough, so little did this move me. I felt nothing at all. Did this mean that I loved her in the past tense?

Her hands stopped mine. "Faith, is this what you want? You look so strange."

How could she see my expression so clearly in this dark room? I did not answer.

Her hands pressed mine against her breast. "You may not believe it after what I've done, but I love you with all my heart. I know how much I've hurt you and I have no way to take it back. There's nothing I can say to change anything. I can only pray that you'll forgive me and that you'll love me again." She sat up and leaned her head wearily on my shoulder.

I sighed. "I hurt inside. It won't go away. I hurt so much I can't feel if I love you or not." This was the truth.

"My love is more than being with you in bed, Faith. I want you physically, so very much, but not if you don't want me that way, too. And I can wait for however long it takes for you to decide. Just don't

147

shut me out, I beg you." Her voice trembled; I pitied her, having been so ill, so close to death.

I put my arms around her and lightly kissed her forehead. It was a sisterly, good-night kiss and she knew it meant good-bye. Strength gone, she slumped against me and I felt her warmth, the remembered softness, her vulnerability; the ice that bound my heart broke into tiny fragments and melted away. With the gentleness of love, I tightened my arms around her and when she raised her face in wonder I kissed her. Softly, tenderly, lovingly, I pressed my lips to hers. Her tears flowed; I tasted their salt, felt her arms hug my waist, her lips hungrily searching mine. I kissed her again and again, lowering her to the bed, raising her gown to kiss her breasts, whatever parts I could reach within the circle of her arms. I kissed her until we were both breathless, like the first time we made love in my soft bed. I entered her with my fingers, my mouth then tasting where my fingers had been. "I love you," she cried and I knew that she did.

Our passion moved like the river, deep and strong . . . and, like a river at flood, the swirling current carried us where it would, finally cresting, leaving us afloat in a quiet, shallow eddy. Entwined, our breath mingling, mouths touching, we kissed softly, without passion. I stroked her back, her hair, held all of her to me, my love free and without condition.

She broke the peaceful silence, "I have to tell you . . ."

"No. Hush now," I whispered, "don't talk, just let me hold you."

"But . . ."

"Tell me in the morning, love. Whatever it is, it'll wait until tomorrow."

She sighed. After a few minutes I heard her breathing deepen into sleep and I felt her steady heartbeat in rhythm with my own. I was alone no longer.

As sleep approached I felt our bodies merge; two became one, and I knew her tiredness, the drain of body and spirit that illness caused and, worse, the throbbing in her shoulders where, my body surging, I had grasped without thinking.

I slept. Dommie moved restlessly and moaned in her sleep, awakening me several times, but I held her and soothed her. Waiting for sleep, I pondered what Dommie had said, wondering if I did, indeed, share her deeper feeling . . . something aside from the passion I felt for her body, the need to share her bed. Even though my heart was newly filled with happiness, I could not be sure.

* * * * *

"Wake up!"

I lowered the sheet an inch or two and peered with one eye at my beautiful Dommie . . . at my heart's desire bending over me.

"Why?"

"Because it's almost noon and you've slept long enough. I've been up for hours." She pulled at the cover, "And the doctor will be here in a few minutes."

I watched her bend closer, her expression loving but her face pale, tired. I brought my arms free and

149

reached for her as she leaned down to touch her lips to mine, her breath then teasing my ear.

"Tonight I'll show you as much as you can handle, little girl."

I moaned aloud. "What if I can't wait until tonight!" There was some truth to this.

"Waiting will make it sweeter." Her lips lightly brushed mine again, then she stood and looked down. "While you were snoring away this morning your Major Claypoole requested our presence at dinner this evening. It's a command performance, I believe."

"Oh, Dommie," I wailed, "I don't want to see that man again! I had enough of him yesterday." I didn't want to be reminded of yesterday or that long ride through the night. Yesterday had hurt too much.

"Well, we can decide about it later. Right now you have to get out of bed and wash yourself. The doctor will be here in a few minutes to see about your feet. Here, put on this gown, love. I don't want that old fool looking at you."

* * * * *

My feet, it seemed, would heal without further attention if I wore soft slippers that didn't aggravate the raw areas, causing infection. I had known this already.

"I can recommend the cobbler across the street." He closed his bag and heaved himself from the stool in front of my chair. "May I congratulate you, ma'am, on your heroic action." He seized my hand, shaking it firmly.

Startled, I jerked loose.

150

Dommie took his arm and hurried him through the door.

"Old fool is right," I grumbled, "what the hell did he mean, Dommie?"

"Sweetheart, we have to talk. Now." Dommie's face was serious. She sat on the stool and looked up at me, "A lot has happened since yesterday morning —"

A knock on the door interrupted; a hotel maid entered pushing a cart laden with enough food for ten people. My stomach lurched at the delicious odors. Somewhat impatiently, Dommie thanked her then hurried her from the room, locking the door behind her. She poured tea for me, heaped food on my plate then poured tea for herself and moved to stand by the window, teacup in her hands, staring down at the street. I knew she was not yet rested, not yet well, but what was causing the sadness that I saw so clearly?

I waited for her to speak but when she didn't I began talking as I chewed. "Let me tell you what I did yesterday." I had to let her know about Major Claypoole, but Dommie interrupted.

"No, love, first let me tell you what happened yesterday." She turned from the window, put her cup on the cart.

"The horses were recognized soon after Henry stabled them, and some deputies arrested Henry . . . after they managed to subdue him. They couldn't make him tell where he got the horses and it wasn't until someone thought to check with the hotel that they found Henry couldn't talk."

Dommie's hands were clenched hard, her knuckles white. Knowing, but not wanting to know, I interrupted, my heart thudding, "Did they hurt him?"

Dommie's green eyes, full of sadness, looked into mine; her voice was tight, controlled, too calm. "They whipped him for a long time before they came here. Malissa and I convinced them that he hadn't done anything wrong and we told them about the *Memphis Queen* and the . . . the pirates." She drew in a deep breath, looking down at her hands. "Then the clerk told them that you were at Major Claypoole's office, that he had sent you there in the hotel carriage. So they calmed down and —"

I interrupted, my voice so choked I could hardly get the words out, "Of course the horses were stolen, I knew that!" I could see Henry, gentle Henry, and the whip slashing through the air. Bile rose in my throat.

Her eyes still on her hands, Dommie said, "Three of the horses belonged to a father and his two sons . . . the men and the horses disappeared almost a year ago on a trip to Helena. One of the other animals has a brand belonging to some people in Corinth and . . ." Dommie's matter-of-fact recitation stopped, her eyes brimmed. She searched her sleeve for a handkerchief, looking helplessly at me. "They beat him because he wouldn't talk . . ." She began sobbing so I leaned to put my arms around her and held her, pressing my lips to her hair.

"I'll kill them." I meant it.

"No." She sniffed. "No more killing, love."

"Come." I put my hands under her arms. "Sit in my lap."

We were silent for a long time.

152

"Now, tell me the rest."

She sighed. "Well, most of this happened in my bedroom down the hall. I had finally fallen asleep and they came crashing into the room and I sat up and . . . and Malissa and I tried to understand, but they were so angry and there were so many of them crowding around . . . I was surprised and confused and didn't know what they wanted. They were all shouting, waving their guns. I thought they were going to take us out and hang us if they didn't shoot us on the spot. But when they finally understood they were very apologetic."

I grunted at this.

"No, really, love, they thought they'd captured a band of murderers."

"They had no right to whip Henry!" I was angry. I should have foreseen something like this, taken care of it before it got out of hand. I was so full of my own pain yesterday morning that I hadn't been thinking straight. "I shouldn't have let it happen!"

Dommie sat up and looked at me, our faces almost touching. She frowned. "You're not responsible for their actions! I forbid you to feel any blame at all!"

I raised my eyebrows. "You forbid?" I asked softly.

Sudden consternation . . . then determination. "Yes! I won't have you feeling guilty when you're not at fault." She pressed her lips to my forehead. "You're the most courageous, the bravest . . . We're all alive only because of you."

At that I grunted again. "Where is he?"

"Malissa has him well in hand. They're staying with a family, some free people of color, somewhere east of here past the Elmwood Cemetery. They're

153

taking good care of him. We're going there as soon as you're dressed." She gave a short laugh. "The deputies didn't give another thought to having whipped Henry. We're the only ones to object."

"But they had no right to do that! Henry's not a slave! Isn't he a free man?"

"Yes, but he's black. To their thinking that made it all right." She paused. "I suppose you could call Henry my half brother-in-law."

I gulped. "I thought something like that. I can tell how much he cares for you. He'd die for you, you know."

"Do you want to know the rest?" Her face was calm, loving.

"Only if you want to tell me." I recalled my confusion that day aboard the *Memphis Queen* when I saw the resemblance between Dommie and Malissa, and thought I knew already some of what Dommie would say.

She said, "I think you should get back in bed where you'll be comfortable and I'll ring to let them know you're ready for your bath."

I slipped under the covers and Dommie tucked me in, then she rang for the tub, unlocked the door, pulled the straight back chair next to the bed and sat primly, facing me with hands folded in her lap.

"Now, my love, we look quite respectable." She grinned at me, her eyes bright. "The ladies LeCompte and O'Neal, cousins and also lovers, are awaiting milady's bath."

It was not long in coming. I sank gratefully into the warm liquid, enjoying the fragrance of scented soap. Dommie turned her chair so that she could watch.

"Malissa is my half sister," she began without preamble, as soon as I had settled in. "My father had Malissa by his mistress, a quadroon, who died of birth complications. Malissa was taken to Ohio to be raised by someone in my father's family but when my father married he had Malissa brought back. His bride, my mother, would have nothing to do with his bastard child and Malissa was to be sent away again. Before that could happen I was born . . . in New Orleans where they were visiting my father's parents, and my mother died that same summer of lung fever."

I sat, not bothering to wash. Dommie knelt by the tub, unpinned my hair, then poured water on my head with the ladle. After raising her cuffs she lathered my hair and began scrubbing. I closed my eyes, already burning from the soap, and listened as she began speaking again.

"My father took Malissa and me to Nashville, to our home, and we were raised together. She's twelve years older and for years I thought she was my mother. I had a governess, whom you'll meet when we get to New Orleans, and I had nurses and tutors but I clung to Malissa."

Dommie rinsed my hair with clean water from the pitcher then returned to her chair. She stared at the ceiling as if to bring memory back. "Malissa has never been a slave, and Henry was free and working for my father as a blacksmith when he and Malissa met. I was about ten when my father and I stood in their wedding. They were free; they could have gone west or to Canada but Father became ill and Malissa wanted to stay. Then their only child, Hank, was born and father died and, well, there we were. Eventually my grandparents brought me to New

155

Orleans, to live with them." Dommie made a face; the memory was obviously unhappy.

"There were thousands of free blacks in New Orleans then," she began again. "Many of them owned homes and businesses and some were land-owning farmers. And Malissa had cousins there. So she and Hank and Henry moved to New Orleans, too, and they were more my family than my grandparents. You see, even if they weren't proud of it, Malissa was their grandchild, too."

Dommie stretched, smiling at me. "I love Malissa. She's my sister and my dearest friend and we've been together all my life."

Now I understood the why of Dommie's involvement with runaway slaves. I thought for a minute. "Well, anything I've wondered about you've answered already, probably."

I stood and Dommie unfolded the towel. "Let me dry you." Her eyes moved over my body, stopping at my breasts, the place where my legs parted, my breasts again. I knew the meaning of her smile, the slow indrawn breath. She began rubbing my back briskly, almost impersonally, and I had to smile when I turned my front to her. She patted my breasts gently with the towel. "I don't want to bruise these. I have plans for them later."

CHAPTER XVI
August, 1862

Later, dressed in clothing provided by the hotel staff, we made our way slowly down the stairs. The people in the lobby buzzed excitedly, watching as we headed for the entrance. I was hobbling painfully and I thought it rude of the other guests to stare. With my feet in this debilitated condition, however, I felt it was acceptable for me to cling to Dommie so I held to her, my breast tight against her arm. Southern ladies seemed to cling to each other a lot. I had a feeling they did this for more than mutual support. Something like Dommie and me perhaps?

I shifted so that Dommie felt that part of me pressing into her. She hissed under her breath and elbowed me sharply.

"I thought you didn't want to make bruises," I hissed back. "The whole lobby just saw you attack me!"

She spoke without moving her lips, "You keep rubbing against me like that and these people will see an attack like they've never imagined!"

She had the sweetest smile; I could tell by looking at the side of her face out of the corner of my eye. "If you poke me again I may get dangerous!"

"You are already the most dangerous person in this town." Her smile broadened as a young man rushed to open the doors for us. She nodded graciously, her arm clamping mine like the jaws of a snapping turtle. We engaged the hotel carriage driven by an ancient Negro. The driver, his black coat too heavy for the season, turned to us. "Will you be going out past the cemetery?"

Nodding, we gaped at him.

"Yes, ma'am." He bowed slightly and turned back to his horse.

"How did he know?" I asked in a low voice as we moved away from the hotel.

Dommie shrugged. "That's just the way it is, love."

"Malissa always seems to know things, too, like what's about to happen or what's not going to happen." I touched Dommie's arm. "She told me you weren't going to die, that you'd get well but I didn't believe her. Maybe if I'd listened to her we might not have gotten into such a mess!"

I heard myself say those words but I didn't really believe them. So I tried to make it clear. "Then again, maybe not. Blest had told me that someone from the camp rode to the wharf every other day or so. And if they had found us huddled in the shed waiting for a boat to stop, Henry would have been shot, we would have been raped, then dumped in the river, shot or not!"

Dommie nodded. "Malissa must have known that. While we were waiting for you, Malissa had Henry move me to that cave in the river bank and cover up all traces that we'd been in the little shack. She told him that you'd come back for us but we needed to move anyway. I was crying because you were gone so long and I wanted to go after you, even if I had to crawl, but Malissa said that if I did . . ."

Forgetting the driver I took Dommie's hands in mine and spoke seriously. "Dommie, if you'd come after me we certainly would have been killed. Thank God Malissa kept you from it!"

It seemed no time until we were off city roads and riding on dirt that wasn't much more than a cow path. It wound between trees and along ditches, passed an occasional shack, crossed pastures and ended at a cemetery fence. The driver followed a faint path around the clustered markers and into a grove of trees that formed a green barrier against a gently sloping hill. And there was Malissa, waiting.

Our driver handed both of us from the carriage with deep bows. He stood grinning as Dommie raced to Malissa's arms. I followed a little more sedately so that I wouldn't walk out of my shoes.

Malissa and I hugged and she whispered, "I see that you two are happy again and that makes me happy, child."

Dommie and I had promised each other that we wouldn't talk about that terrible night, now that the hurt between us had been healed, but that didn't mean I had to stop thinking about what had happened and about my part in it. And I knew that Dommie hadn't meant to harm me. In that one terrible moment, as weak and ill as she was, she didn't really see that it was me at her side, just that someone had finally caught her as she galloped through the night and she was fighting to get free. My stubborn pride was injured and so I deliberately wounded Dommie in the cruellest way I knew. I took away my love and then, like a child, blamed her because I felt deserted.

Arm in arm, the three of us walked to the small wooden house. I saw Henry, shirtless, waiting on the narrow porch. He reached for my hand and held it in both of his for a long moment while Malissa and Dommie beamed.

Henry's back was slashed raw but a homemade salve of crushed vegetable matter and rendered fat had been applied, soothing and preventing the wounds from festering. Henry would recover but he would carry scars for the rest of his life.

* * * * *

Major Claypoole was grim at dinner. Underneath his very polite social behavior was a man who wanted to lash out at something. We were joined by one of

160

his aides and both of them tried unsuccessfully to hide their gloom.

Dommie, however, sparkled. She had done some folding and pinning and had made a dress which I thought showed entirely too much bosom. The men obviously didn't think so because their gaze was riveted there most of the evening.

My mother's emerald necklace, a deeper green than Dommie's eyes, flashed as the light from the chandeliers caught each breathing movement of her breast. Matching earrings emphasized the soft outline of her white throat, the delicate hollows formed when she turned her head to give attention to one or the other of us. The Major and the aide were smitten.

"You gentlemen seem downcast. Could the news of Bull Run have anything to do with it?" The entire town was buzzing about the rout; the hotel maids had been gleeful and talkative.

"You are very discerning, Ma'am. Yes, we had disturbing news this morning, as I see you've heard also. Our armies were roundly defeated . . ." He patted Dommie's hand. "You ladies don't want to hear distressing war news."

Obviously, he was not thinking that what was bad news to him might not be to us.

Our meal was delicious and I ate some of everything in sight but Dommie merely played with the food on her plate. She sipped a little wine, drank water, and kept the two men charmed.

She was delightfully feminine, her beauty awesome, green eyes flashing as she laughed at some comment, her long, dark lashes shadowing her cheek when she looked down, a tiny strand of jet black hair escaping to form a soft curl against the whiteness of her skin. Her slim fingers caressed the stem of her glass, a habit I remembered well. She was entirely desirable. There was nothing coy or coquettish in her manner as she captivated the men; she was a mature woman who knew how to use a woman's enchantment.

The table was cleared but still we lingered. It was apparent the men would have stayed all night. During the meal, to my great embarrassment, perfect strangers had approached our table to congratulate Dommie and me on our heroic stand against the river pirates. I wanted to accuse the Major of spreading the story but knew that the deputies and the hotel staff were the ones to blame.

Dommie finally asked the question. "When will your men return from the river, Major?"

"We should hear from them by morning, Ma'am. I will come personally to give you an accounting."

I barely refrained from saying, "I bet you will, you ass!" Instead, I smiled sweetly at Dommie and said pointedly, "I'm rather tired, Cousin, I think I'll go to my room."

The gentlemen rose as I did. Dommie rose a moment later, both of the men almost falling over the table to hold her chair. She extended her hand to the Major who took it and bowed deeply, as did the Captain. She was gracious and completely composed, not speaking, merely nodding somewhat regally, her lips forming a little half-smile. They walked us to the stairs and watched as we ascended; Dommie moving gracefully while I hobbled from step to step, clutching the rail in support.

I was going to go into my own room but Dommie had a bulldog's grip on my arm. "No you don't," she said, pulling me down the hall.

Once inside her sitting room we faced each other.

"You know you made me jealous, don't you?" I said softly, knowing I had to make my feelings clear.

Her voice was hushed. "I wasn't trying to."

"You don't have to show me that you can have anyone you want . . . I've always known that." I pulled her to me, holding her close. "I already love you with all my heart, Dommie, and I always will. Please don't do that to me anymore."

Her face was half-hidden and I almost couldn't hear, she spoke so softly: "It just got out of hand. They were both so simple."

I thought I also needed to say the other thing that had been bothering me most of the evening. "Would you rather have a man? Am I just entertainment for you until you marry again?"

She moved back and looked at me, astonishment on her face. "Why are you asking me that?" Then she took my face in her hands, her eyes filled with pain. "Of course not! No, love, no! Can't you understand that it's you I want, not some man? Oh, dear God, I thought you believed me." She drew in a deep breath. "I've hurt you again, haven't I? You wouldn't ask me that if you were sure of my love." She started to turn away. "I love you too much to keep hurting you this way!"

"So you're going to leave me?" I was smiling because I knew she couldn't and because her answer had freed my heart from unbearable pain. I held her arm.

She saw my wide grin. Surprised, she took a moment to speak. "No, little girl," she snapped, her green eyes flashing, "I'm going to cut out my tongue!"

I pulled her into my arms and whispered that cutting out her tongue would create a hardship when we were kissing and making love, not to mention the unimportant disadvantages.

"Dommie, listen to me." I spoke slowly. "Everything was so simple in the beginning. We loved each other and were going to make a home together in New Orleans and raise Elsas and Antoinette and live happily ever after. And I never really thought beyond that, or even how we were going to get that far. I think I've cried more in the last few days than I've done in all my twenty-three years, and you've done your share, too. We're doing things and saying things to each other that neither of us mean."

She nodded, I could feel her head moving against me.

"Tonight I got jealous. It's that simple. Both of those men wanted you, I could see it. And you were egging them on, I could see that, too. But I don't ever want to hurt you. I love you."

She raised her beautiful face. "I love you, too. And we are going to have a life together . . . if you still want me."

I tightened my arms. "Need you ask?' I whispered.

"Would you trade me for a man?" She was very serious.

I had to laugh. "You know I wouldn't."

"Well, love, I won't trade you if you won't trade me!"

We kissed to seal the pact.

164

Her nearness stirred sensations that had been dormant for all of my life before her. I knew those years were but a prelude, a preparation. When her fingers had touched mine that day, that long-ago day on the steps of her home, and her eyes smiled into mine, I found the future, and my fulfillment.

We helped each other undress and, naked, entered our bed. I turned to her and raised on an elbow. "I want to love you the way it feels good to me. I want to touch you with my lips." And I kissed her, a slow, soft kiss. "I want to touch you with my tongue." I outlined her lips with my tongue then I leaned and outlined a nipple. "I want to be close to you." I raised myself above her then lowered my body to hers. "I want to feel you soft and warm against me . . ."

She moved her legs apart so that mine were on the mattress between hers. I drew my legs up and knelt, looking down at her.

"I've been thinking about you and how you make me feel. I can get excited just thinking." I leaned and kissed her, feeling her tongue on mine. "Do you get that way thinking of me?"

She pulled me all the way down so that my body met hers again; her hands caressed my back, her fingers moving over familiar paths. Our mouths joined and I pressed my breasts into hers. She shifted her hips, raising them against me. "Try me." It was a low, inviting whisper. I moved to her side and let my hand trail slowly down her body. Gently I searched between her legs. I found wetness.

"Ahhh . . ." Which of us made that sound?

I moved off the bed and helped Dommie turn so that she was lying on the edge, her knees up, her heels at the turn of the mattress. I put a pillow on the bedstool and knelt to kiss the inside of her thighs, my touch light. I found her soft opening with my tongue and stroked gently, not entering but moving in circles, spreading the velvet lips slightly. I kissed and kissed, my hands now reaching to touch her breasts, to fondle the smooth, silken mounds, to tease the hardness I found there.

"Faith," Dommie pleaded, hands closing hard on mine, hips lifting, inviting me into her. She stretched her legs to encase my shoulders, the soft weight imprisoning me between her smooth thighs, holding me in place.

I heard her rapid breathing, the sharp intake of breath as I sucked, pressing my lips against the wetness. I moved my tongue faster, making her hips jerk as I stroked through the moisture. Then, heart pounding, I entered her; my tongue slipped between soft walls. My back was arched, my own breathing loud and harsh, the sound filling my head. I heard her gasp my name and I pressed deeper, my hands pulling her hard against my face, my own throat making helpless noises. She tensed, breath suspended, body rigid, hands reaching for my head, to hold it tight in place. I tasted the rush of fluid and knew the shuddering of her body as the spasms claimed her . . . then felt her breathing begin, her body relax.

I remained between her thighs, my hands holding hers, waiting for her to release me. Then, when she turned longways on the bed, I lay next to her, using the sheet to wipe her wetness from my face. Her hand searched for mine. "I want to love you, little girl, but I need . . . a moment to recover."

"Do you still love me?" I had to hear it.

She took in enough air to be able to answer. "Yes," she said simply.

"Then go to sleep now. Put your head on my shoulder and go to sleep."

"But . . ."

"We'll have time for me," I whispered, "You need rest." I held my arms around her as she drifted into sleep.

She's too tired, I thought, and she's still not well. I've not given her enough time to recover. She's not eating and I don't help any, always wanting to be in bed with her. I remembered her sagging helplessly against the wagon's side, unable to stand without Malissa's support. I thought of the spoon that had dropped from her hand, the small spoon that was too heavy for her to lift. I wanted her to be strong again, and she was trying but there had not been enough time.

I held my brave and beautiful baby, my arms gentle around her so that if she woke she'd feel safe in the circle of my love.

CHAPTER XVII
Monday, September 11, 1862

The food on our breakfast cart tasted even better than it smelled. I was filling my plate for the second time.

"You're not eating." I was very concerned.

"No, I'm not really hungry."

"I want you to eat. Please?"

She sighed and gave me a little smile, "If you say so."

Dommie's face was still pale, with dark circles under her eyes. I cursed myself. She had simply done too much too soon. "Did the doctor give you any medicine, Dommie?"

She evaded my eyes. "I don't remember."

"That means he did. Where is it?"

"Must you?"

"Is it in your dresser?"

She made a face, shrugging. I went into the bedroom and opened drawers, withdrawing from one a medicine bottle full of dark brown liquid.

"This is a tonic, isn't it?" I said, showing it to her. "Maybe iron to help build your strength?"

She made another face. "It'll make me throw up, I promise you."

I thought about that, recalling the terrible vomiting that had gone on for so long. I knelt, pleading. "Dommie, you need something to help you get stronger. Please?"

She nodded, sighing.

"And will you eat something, too?"

Another nod, another sigh.

"Do you want your medicine first or do you want to eat first?"

This time her sigh was huge. "Medicine, I think. Then tea." She looked piteously at me. "Maybe the tea will help kill the taste."

"All right," I said cheerfully. "Medicine first then tea. Tea and a biscuit." Smiling broadly for Dommie's benefit, I poured a spoonful of the foul-smelling liquid and held it to her mouth.

"Remember on the boat, my love? I'm going to hold this in front of your face 'till you open your

169

mouth and swallow!" Her mouth was turned down and she looked at the spoon with the same expression she'd use if it had been a rattlesnake poised to strike at her throat. How could I be so cruel? Relenting, I started to lower my arm but Dommie touched my wrist, steadying my hand.

Another grimace but she guided the spoon to her mouth. Then she grabbed for the water glass, sputtering, trying to get the liquid to go down. Finally, choking, she looked at me with huge eyes. "I thought you said you loved me!"

"I did and I do," I said softly. "Now drink your tea and eat!"

"You have no pity," she sniffed, dabbing at her mouth with the napkin.

I handed her the tea. "What I have is love, deep and abiding, but I won't have you getting sick again." I could not bear it if you did, I thought, I simply could not bear it if you were hurting again. "How much of that stuff are you supposed to take in a day?"

"One spoon," she answered promptly.

"Dommie!"

"Two spoons?" Her eyes searched the air around me.

"You're impossible!" But I was grinning.

"Oh?" Now her eyes widened as they met mine, "I wasn't impossible last night was I?"

"Well, no," I admitted, "you were delicious."

* * * * *

We were dressed and in the lobby when Major Claypoole and his aide arrived at the hotel. Somberly, he suggested that we meet in the dining room, perhaps have tea or coffee while we talked.

My heart sank at his words. With a sense of foreboding so sharp I could taste it welling up in my throat, I walked arm in arm with Dommie, preceding the men into the huge, busy room. As they seated us my fear became so tangible that I couldn't make words come out of my mouth. A huge chasm was opening in front of me and I felt myself slipping toward the edge.

Dommie was watching my face; frowning, she reached for my hand and covered it with her own, pressing mine hard against the table.

Her eyes cold, her voice sharp, she said, "You did not capture all of them, did you, Major?"

I could see that he did not want to tell us what he had to tell us. "No, we surprised them but, in the confusion, some escaped."

The waiter came but Dommie waved him away.

"Who?" I managed. "Who . . .?" Dommie's hand gripped mine painfully.

"Their leader, Miss O'Neal, the man you called Lonnie — Alonzo Forbes Bell, to use the name on his wanted posters. He and two others. We have captured all but Bell."

"How?" When my heart is held by fear I seem to be capable of action but not of speech.

The Major would not look directly at me. He spoke to the tablecloth. "Three men on horseback fled deeper into the swamp, managing to evade us in the confusion. My men could not follow but we surrounded the area and captured two of them as they rode out to firm ground. These two told my officers that their leader, Bell, was the third man."

"Do you have any idea where he is now, Major?" Dommie knew, as well as the Major, what Bell's escape could mean. Neither of them, however, could realize to the fullest just how threatening this was.

"Yes." The Major seemed relieved. "We had a report of him earlier. He was seen heading south on the river road. It was a positive identification. We've sent his description as far as New Orleans. Unless he hides out in the swamps, we'll have him if he reaches there or any other city between. I don't think you have anything to fear, Miss O'Neal." He sounded sincere, as if he believed what he was saying.

"Major, you'll let us know when you hear anything definite?" Dommie was ready to leave, her hand still clamping mine.

I found my tongue, "Was there a little girl? With red hair?"

The Major shook his head slowly. "No, Miss O'Neal, no children. Several women but no children."

I wanted to ask about Miss Lester but my voice failed again.

Dommie lifted my hand. "Let's go, darling."

We stood and the Major looked directly at me for the first time. I suppose he meant it as a compliment when he said, "If you had been with us, Miss O'Neal, we may have done a better job."

* * * * *

The chasm had claimed me. Back in Dommie's suite, I sat on the edge of the velvet chair, Dommie paced. I could not seem to get my thoughts together, could not climb the slippery walls back to reason. My hands were tightly clasped to hide their trembling from Dommie.

"Please stop pacing. I can't think!"

Dommie knelt, putting her hands over mine, squeezing.

"He'll come for me. For you. He's not stupid like the others. He won't be caught, not by anyone. He'll be here. I know he'll be here, and he'll kill us. I've done too much and . . . and now I don't even have a gun." I pulled my hands from Dommie's, gripped them together again. "We won't see him, but he's going to kill us."

"I will not have you afraid like this." Dommie's face was set, her voice cold. "That murdering swine will never touch you. Never!" In her eyes I saw again the steely determination that had enabled her to ride through darkness to give freedom to those she didn't even know. "We are neither of us afraid of your Mr. Bell!" She stood and pulled me to my feet. "Now get up, we're going shopping!"

But first we had to go to my room to get money from under the mattress. Dommie guided me down the hall, her hand squeezing mine. She made sure the door was locked then fished out one of the sacks and emptied it on the bed.

"Dommie, how much is that?"

She was reaching under the mattress again. "I think each sack is worth about twenty-five hundred, so there's something over thirty thousand in all. That's as much gold as Sidney could handle at one time. It was against the law for him to do this, you know. The Federals were forcing us to take printed money but Sidney gave me what he could in gold and the rest is a draft somewhere in one of these sacks. I suppose in New Orleans they'll cover the draft with paper money but there's nothing we can do about it."

I picked up one of the coins and admired the sharp liberty head outline. "Is this money the reason you didn't want me traveling with you?"

Dommie emptied another sack. "In a way, darling. Too many people in the bank knew about this gold and we ran a very real risk of being robbed . . . killed before we could get out of town or jailed by the soldiers. Doing this was foolish but Sidney said this was the only way if I wanted to keep any money at all. Ah," she said, emptying another sack, "this is what I want!" She gathered a handful of five, ten and twenty dollar pieces. "We don't want to draw attention with too many of the larger denominations, do we, little girl?"

"I love it when you call me that."

"I love to call you that!" Her arms reached and we held each other.

I kissed her eyelids and the tip of her nose then I helped her shove the gold far under the mattress and kissed her again in a tight embrace before leaving the room.

* * * * *

We could both see that Memphis was not a city devastated by the Union takeover. Since the brief river battle the city was full of Union soldiers, but business was going on as usual in spite of martial law; better than usual, we learned, what with everyone almost openly smuggling to the Confederates.

The municipal government was still functioning but our slow walk showed us a town that was filthy and not only crowded with soldiers but with refugees, both white and black, their strident voices loud in the streets; the streets themselves were littered, smelling of all manner of refuse and steaming hot in the blazing summer sun.

Because of my feet, so painful in ill-fitting shoes, Dommie and I inched our way around the square, eyeing with interest the shops which lined the streets. Dommie commented on the acrid odor which filled our nose with every vagrant breeze.

I explained, "They burned the cotton to keep it out of Union hands, hundreds of bales, and it still smells."

"I'm only grateful my cotton wasn't burned, too. Did you know that we were supposed to burn our own crop to keep it from going to the North? My neighbors organized armed patrols with orders to burn whatever hadn't been already." Dommie gave a short laugh. "So if I didn't burn it or my neighbors didn't, the Federal soldiers could confiscate it and pay paper dollars or not pay anything at all." Dommie shook her head. "I think we're lucky to have gotten out of it. I only hope Hank can finish picking before some ass rides by with a torch!"

She was determined to take my mind off Lonnie, so she dragged me into the first dressmaking shop we saw and kept us there so that the dressmaker could measure both of us and display the fabrics that were available.

There were soldiers on the walk and in the streets and a few stood peering into the window, but they meant no harm. They simply had nothing to do and

Memphis didn't offer much recreation for idle men. I made sure that Lonnie wasn't one of the men looking through the glass.

"Now, shoes." Dommie held my arm as we continued around the square and we both nodded amicably when some young soldier touched his hat to us. "Yankees aren't so bad," Dommie said, squeezing my arm. "Especially mine."

The cobbler was pleased to take an order. I drew a pattern for the design I wanted and Dommie ordered a matching pair for herself.

Then I watched as Dommie stood, her skirt raised ankle-high, so the shoemaker could make an outline of her foot. Dommie's waist was tiny, her form slender and her shoulders softly rounded. Her bosom, though flattened by the tight bodice, was full and, as she drew her shawl aside, I could see the delicate shape of each nipple through the thin cloth. I smiled at this; she was not wearing a corset again! The gown hugged her waist, long folds concealing the curve of her hips and her slim, well-shaped legs. My mind, I found, was finally concerned with something other than Lonnie.

I bought a pair of soft, ready-made slippers and wore them from the shop. Blessed relief! I could walk again!

"Are you hungry, love?" Dommie's arm was through mine, her hand firm.

"I could eat." A carriage stopped at the curb . . . my heart thudded until it emptied its three ladies then moved away.

"Then let's go back to the hotel. I think I could eat something, too. Maybe soup and cold ham . . . some of that delicious smoked ham . . . that's what I want . . ." She sensed that I had relaxed and seemed pleased that her efforts to distract me had been successful. I would try harder to conceal my fear so as not to spoil her day. I only looked behind me twice as we walked back to the hotel.

We sat long at our meal then made our way upstairs, and as soon as the hall door closed behind us, we embraced. Dommie walked into my arms and I held her. We stood without speaking, happy to be able to touch, happy to be together. And I was happy we were still alive.

"I need to get out of this dress," Dommie informed me. "Help me with these buttons . . ."

"I know you haven't a stitch on under that dress. Are you trying to start something, my dear?"

"Maybe," Dommie answered, smiling, "maybe not. But this dress is too tight on my shoulders, love . . ."

I unbuttoned and when I pulled the bodice down I saw that her shoulders were, indeed, very red and newly irritated. "Do you think we'll ever recover from this trip?" I asked, kissing the hurt places to make them well.

"I think we'll all recover the minute we get on the boat. It's this place. We've had only trouble since we got here. Even while we were on our way here!"

I knew she was thinking about Spirit. "Tell you what, you put on your gown while I go collect newspapers. We'll read for a while, rest, have our supper sent up and then go to bed early."

I kissed her before I left, not to miss an opportunity, and walked down the hall to the stairs. Before I reached the staircase I had the feeling that someone was behind me. Whirling, my breath catching, I scanned the hall. It was empty. But the feeling had been so strong that my skin crawled as I took each cautious step down to the lobby.

Hastily, I collected a few papers, most of them from distant cities and several days old, then hurried to our room, looking over my shoulder several times before I reached the door.

Dommie was in a nightgown, her bare toes peeking from under the hem, and she hugged me, crushing the papers between us. "We'll have a wonderful evening, love. Just the two of us." She pulled back the window drapes, "See, our afternoon shower. We'll be cool and comfortable and together."

No! No! Close the drapes, my mind screamed. But I said nothing.

I worked hard at concealing my fear. We read, ate our supper from the cart, ordered tea for later and enjoyed the slight cooling breeze brought by the rain.

I told myself that Lonnie was hiding deep in the swamp or, better, already jailed or killed by the soldiers or the deputies. Of course he was. I told myself that he was nowhere near, then I flinched at every noise, almost jumped out of the chair when the maid came for the cart and brought our tray of tea and once was on the verge of telling Dommie to hush so I could listen for noises in the hall.

We lit our lamps and I scrutinized each shadow that moved as the light fluctuated.

"Darling, are you all right?" Dommie could not help but pick up hints from my behavior.

"Of course I'm all right," I lied. "I'm just thinking that you didn't take your medicine this evening."

"Please, baby, can we start tomorrow? I promise to be good. Tomorrow?"

Ordinarily I would have insisted she take the medicine but I didn't want to go into the bedroom to fetch the bottle. I could not bring myself to enter that dark place carrying a lamp that illuminated me more than the room. This was irrational, but I was too frightened to be rational and I didn't want Dommie to be afraid, too. One of us trembling at each sound was enough.

I was sitting, staring at the door, and without conscious thought was evaluating each sound, when Dommie touched me on the shoulder. I jerked as if I'd been shot.

"Let's go to bed."

No! I didn't want to go to bed! "Yes," I said and rose from the chair, Dommie's hand in mine.

"We'll leave the windows and the bedroom door open so we can catch the breeze."

No, I thought again. Positively no! "All right," I answered. We were, after all, on the second floor. He'd have to be a fly to climb in one of our windows. And our hall door was locked. I'd checked it to be sure.

We left a lamp burning low in the sitting room and got into bed. Dommie began touching me, kissing me. I listened to the rustle of the bed clothing. Was it loud enough to cover any other sounds?

Her hands, insistent, caught my attention. More, they claimed my whole body. "Do you want me to love you, little girl?"

Maybe because I was preoccupied — I really can't say — our lovemaking was different. No less intense

179

but different . . . softer, slower, building almost quietly to that moment of fire. And that, too, came as a lightning surge, catching me without warning, my body arching, surprised. There was little of the frantic passion we usually shared, our hearts thudding, limbs rigid with desire.

Dommie moved from me, lay by my side, her voice low, pleased, "I don't think I've ever loved you like that."

"No," I answered, "this is the first time. But I liked it that way. It was so good I thought for a minute I was going to die."

"Don't say that, even in jest!"

I turned to her, all my fears forgotten, vanished in the rush of love that I felt. "Let me love you now?"

"Yes, love me now. I want you so very much!"

"You have me. For all of our lives . . . you have me."

CHAPTER XVIII
Monday, September 1, 1862

I pulled the bedroom door almost shut behind me. No need to wake Dommie because I couldn't sleep. Still drained by illness as she was, sleep was her best means to recover, sleep and the gentle loving we had shared a few minutes ago. I smiled as I crossed the room, remembering Dommie and the loving.

My book was still on the table. I sat and turned up the lamp, intending to read until I became sleepy.

Settling back, I opened the book and turned slightly so as to benefit most from the light.

There was no sound. He moved as quietly as a shadow. I heard nothing but in the few seconds before he touched me, I felt him in the room. I felt his presence behind me and I dropped the book to my lap, intending to leap from the chair. He had me before I could move.

One arm forced my head back against the chair, my neck twisting, my breath cut off; the other hand clamped something hard against my mouth so that I could make no sound. I struggled, trying to lever myself upwards to overturn the chair, but he tightened his grip around my neck, jerking his elbow hard under my chin. I clutched at his arm, pulling at the fabric of his coat but I might as well have clawed at bricks.

I felt no terror, no fear, only an anger that fueled my struggles. Soon, though, my lungs screamed for air but his arm constricted my throat. I felt my hands falling away from his arm and saw great bursts of light when I squeezed my eyes shut to make one last effort . . . then darkness.

Awareness returned with a rush. I opened my eyes.

"I'm glad you're conscious, Miss O'Neal, I was beginning to think that I had caused some permanent damage." He smiled at me and patted my hands which were now tied together in my lap. "Let me know if you're uncomfortable. We have a long night ahead, my dear."

I looked into a face of total madness. He had bound my wrists tightly with a silken scarf, much more effective than rope, and my mouth had been stuffed with cloth so that I couldn't move my tongue, couldn't swallow. Another scarf around my face held the gag in place and was pulled painfully taut so that it pinched my cheeks, cutting into the sides of my mouth and holding my teeth apart. He had also roped my ankles, each to a leg of the chair. Another rope crossed my throat and one was just under my breasts, pulled tight and probably knotted behind the chair. I was trussed like a Christmas pig.

There was no way I could communicate with him. Raising and lowering my eyebrows would only make me look foolish so I sat, unmoving. Whatever was to happen would be up to him anyway.

"Miss O'Neal," he began quietly, "you have, by your efforts alone, destroyed my life. I have been forced to flee my home, losing all my worldly goods to fire, losing my companions to death and capture . . ." He patted my hands again. "I owe you a debt which I will pay tonight."

He pulled the straight chair in front of me and sat so that we were facing, knee to knee, and then he pulled a knife from his boot. It was long and slim and pointed and caught the light from the lamp as he held it in front of my face. "I was going to cut you with this, my dear, until I felt the debt had been paid but I don't think you care about personal discomfort, do you?"

He touched the knife point to my neck, just under my left ear, and involuntarily I moved my head. A little jab and the point went into my flesh. I felt pain, yes. My mouth watered, instantly absorbed by the wad of cloth. I needed to swallow but I couldn't so I said, "You bastard." The sound came out as a grunt, a grunt of anger.

His smile was demented. "See, you didn't really mind that, did you?" Now the point pressed upward against my left breast. "Or this?"

The point slid through the material of my gown and into me. I twisted and screamed into the gag; not from pain but from pure rage. We went through the same routine on the right side. I felt myself trying to jerk away but it was only a reflex. There was no place I could move that would be out of his reach and he told me so.

"You can't escape, my dear, not really." And he jabbed lightly again, this time catching the fabric and slicing upward so that my gown fell open, slicing some of me in the process. He looked at my bosom carefully, as if I were something he considered buying. "These are lovely, Miss O'Neal." With his free hand he stroked my breasts, pinching each nipple, smiling as I tried to move away from the pain. "Ah, yes, quite lovely," he murmured. Then, smiling, he said, "Your cousin, however, is more to my fancy."

I howled. I lunged at him, twisting, rearing, straining against the bonds. He sat, smiling as I struggled, listening with approval to the whimpering sounds that came from my throat, futile noises that helped me not at all.

"I watched you in bed tonight. You and your cousin. Now I know why you were so anxious to return to her." His eyes were deep hollow wells. "I saw what you did together and it moved me." He touched the point of the knife to the hollow at my throat. "It moved me as I haven't been moved in some time." The point lightly grazed my flesh, stinging as it sliced downward. "So much, in fact, that I'll have you watch as I violate her. That, I believe, will be more punishment for you than this . . ." And he sliced again, slowly, lightly, almost lovingly.

I heaved at the rope, twisting against the chair, rage blinding me, making tears fall.

"Ah, yes, I thought that would catch your attention. You'll enjoy watching what I do to your cousin . . . Afterwards you can watch her die."

He slipped the knife back into his boot and stood . . . And with a crashing roar his chest sprouted a rosette of bright blood directly in the center. There was another roar and a second rosette burst next to the first. Lonnie's back hit the wall with a thud, overturning the chair, and he slid slowly to the floor, to sit upright with one leg outstretched, his foot almost touching mine, eyes half-lidded, hands relaxed on his thighs. My breath stopped. I could not turn my eyes from the liquid smear on the wall above his head.

Dommie's face appeared, blotting out the wet, red ribbon. She knelt, choking at the sight of my blood-soaked lap. I watched her turn and impatiently twist Lonnie's leg so that she could reach in his boot for the knife. Her hands gentle, she began cutting the knot that held the scarf to my face. It fell away and she pulled the wadded cloth from my mouth. I started gagging but it was necessary for me to talk. My tongue was so dry it stuck to the inside of my mouth.

"He was going to hurt you," I croaked. "He was going to kill you!"

"No, he wasn't." Her voice was tight. "I woke and heard something, so I tiptoed to the door and saw . . . and saw him." She had cut the rope that bound me to the chair. Now she held my hands and began cutting at a silken knot.

"I couldn't shoot him because you were almost directly between us."

There was more than one knot. Her hands were trembling and she was drawing deep breaths.

"I was afraid if he saw me he'd kill you outright but if I tried to shoot him over your head he might have fallen on you with the knife and he'd be dead but so would you . . ."

The last knot gave and my hands were loose, numb but free, and I tried but couldn't lift them from my lap.

There was a great pounding on the door, loud voices. Dommie began slicing at the bonds that held my legs. Something hard crashed against wood and I heard the door slam back against the wall at the same time that my legs were freed.

Dommie, still kneeling in front of me, did not look up. "Get a doctor."

Then she leaned and pulled me to her, her arms gentle around me. I rested my head on hers.

* * * * *

They were gone. The doctor, Major Claypoole, his aide and many soldiers, two deputies, the hotel manager and assorted guests who had heard either the gunshots or the commotion made by those who had come to our aid.

Someone, the doctor perhaps, had turned down all but one lamp and its gentle flickering created a softness, a haziness that made the boundaries of the

186

room draw together in shadow. We had been moved to another suite and we were alone.

"Little girl?" She leaned toward me where I lay on the bed, her voice gentle, softer than snowflakes.

"Me?" I asked.

"I love you," she said.

For the space of two breaths I wondered how to say what I was thinking. Then I decided she would want me to be myself, not hold back. "Get in with me."

"What?"

"Get in bed with me."

"Are you out of your mind?"

"It has nothing to do with my mind."

"Sweetheart, I can't do that!"

"Why?"

"Because you're hurt."

"I'm not that much hurt. If you don't get in with me I'm going back to my own room. If I have to sleep alone I might as well do it there."

"But I'm going to stay here, right next to you all night."

"I want you next to me in bed, not in that chair." An idea struck me. "If you won't get in with me then I'll get in the chair with you." I lifted the cover and moved my feet to the side of the bed.

"Don't do that!"

She was smiling as she held the cover and eased herself next to me. I had to shift more to the middle of the bed but, contrary to what the doctor predicted, movement did not cause any great discomfort.

The old fool, as Dommie called him, finally did get to look at me . . . and feel me, too. She had stood next to him and held the basin as he cleaned away

187

blood, wiping my front so as to see the damage. I could hardly believe it but there really wasn't too much. A few light slices but I've had cat scratches worse. Where Lonnie poked the knife tip under my breasts and beneath my ear was tender, painful to the touch but not deep. There was a lot of blood which had made me look half dead but no lasting injury.

The doctor had said, "It's a miracle, Miss O'Neal. Almost as if he didn't intend to hurt you. Of course he may have been saving the worst for later, after he had, ah, dealt with Mrs. LeCompte." This was Major Claypoole's thinking as well.

But I had looked into those demented eyes and I knew what Lonnie meant to do to me after I had watched Dommie die. The light scratches would have become deep, mortal wounds, the knife point slowly inching into my flesh, grinding, raking bone. Lonnie would have known how to make it last.

"Rest, Miss O'Neal," the doctor had said. "And don't move around too much. I'll see you in the morning."

"How much," I now whispered, "how much moving around is too much, do you think?"

"Anything you have in mind is too much. I'll hold you, love, but that's all."

"That's really all I want . . . just hold me."

We lay together in the quiet room and I found that her loving arms, close around me, were all the comfort I could ever want or need.

"Will you always hold me?" I asked. I had to know that her arms would be there for me when I needed them.

"Yes, I'll always hold you." She knew what I meant.

I wanted to wrap myself around her but found that I was much more comfortable the way I was. Comfortable but not sleepy. I kept seeing Lonnie's face.

"Dommie?"

"Ummm?"

"Where did you get the gun?"

"I kept the one you gave me. Malissa told me to."

"Does she read minds or something?"

"Sometimes I think so."

"Does it bother you that you killed a man tonight? If you feel like crying or talking, I'm here, you know. Better than anyone, I can understand how you feel."

She took in a deep breath and let it out slowly. "I'm not sure how I feel. When I think of the way he was hurting you I'm inclined to find his body and shoot him some more just to make sure he's dead." She sighed again. "That isn't the Christian way to feel but if I hadn't shot him it would be the two of us dead now. If I had to put a word to the way I feel it would probably be . . ." A pause while she considered. "Victorious, I feel victorious! Now, go to sleep!"

CHAPTER XIX
September, 1862

The next day while I was supposed to be recuperating, I watched Dommie to see if she was having second thoughts about shooting Lonnie, but her countenance remained serene, untroubled. She looked better; her face had color and she didn't appear as tired. Certainly she was not suffering pangs of conscience because of killing him.

It occurred to me that thousands of good men had died already in this war; thousands more would perish if the fighting continued to rage across the land. But these legions were sworn soldiers, using cannon and sword against those equally armed. Annihilation of an enemy is, in wartime, planned military strategy; the ensuing deaths are expected, the lines are plugged with fresh new bodies, the battles go on. Lonnie, however, had killed those who had no defense. Men, women and children had been parted from this life to give Lonnie and his men profit or amusement. Lonnie had deserved to die. All of those murderers had deserved to die.

I thought of Miss Lester. Even if she had escaped with her life, how could she return to a normal existence after the degradations heaped upon her by those men? I must remember to ask Major Claypoole for the names of the women who were rescued. Remembering Miss Lester's sweet face, I hoped she would be among them.

At breakfast we received a note from Major Claypoole informing us that we were due several rewards: one for killing Lonnie, one for locating the camp, two for finding the whereabouts of certain missing people. He would be happy to handle these at our convenience. "Sure he would," I told Dommie. "He wants to get another look at you."

"Then let's write to thank him and tell him to give the money to charity. We certainly don't need to profit from other people's misery, do we?"

"Well, no. But I don't think it's a good idea to turn down money, either. Two days ago I didn't know how I was going to pay for my room. Maybe we should —"

Dommie broke in, "Were you really going to leave me?"

"No! Why are you even asking?"

"I just need to be reassured." Dommie was eating the last of an absolute mountain of food, more than I had seen her eat since Nashville.

"What reassures me is seeing you eat." I wondered if I would have to watch every word out of my mouth from now on so as not to remind her that I had, indeed, planned to leave her. I put down my napkin. "Let's both bathe. I need to get clean from last night." The doctor had wiped my front and Dommie had wiped a little more but I still felt crusty in places the cleaning hadn't reached.

"No bath but I'll sponge you."

I thought about being sponged. I liked the thought.

* * * * *

Major Claypoole saw us to the wharf and to our stateroom aboard the *Mississippi Star*. Dommie and I were fashionably gowned, our hats the latest style, our parasols dainty; we were both demurely shawl-covered and properly appreciative of the Major's concern.

I looked upon the Major with more favor after he had brought drafts covering eleven thousand dollars in reward money to our door. "Yes," he answered Dommie's question, "the rewards were offered in gold, both of them, but I don't know how these bank drafts will be paid in New Orleans. My office, you understand, has no money with which to honor the terms of payment but you can be sure that your bank in New Orleans will accept these at face value." I think he was shocked that Dommie had even asked whether we'd collect in gold or paper. Ladies weren't supposed to think about money, neither specie nor the printed kind.

The ship's captain was, he stated, honored to have us with him. Hastily the Major assured us that we would not suffer the same fate as that aboard the *Memphis Queen*. "I certainly hope not," Dommie whispered to me as the men bowed themselves out of the room. "I don't think I could go through that again!"

Dommie turned the door lock and leaned back, looking at me, smiling that special smile. She removed her hat, flicking it across the room to the bed. "We're now where we should have been weeks ago. Think we can take up where we would have been then if not for being robbed, kidnapped, ill, abandoned, shot at, knifed . . ."

I hushed her with my lips. I undressed her. I removed my own clothing. We took up where we would have been if not for all those things. Our trip downriver, on the clean, sweet-smelling sheets I had dreamed about that day long ago in the swamp, was everything I could have wished for.

* * * * *

Major Claypoole had wired ahead to reserve accommodations for us at the Saint Charles Hotel but when we reached New Orleans, we found the hotel to be headquarters for General Butler and his staff. This was unacceptable to Dommie, and I wasn't too happy about being housed with the Union army, either. We were graciously received by the manager of the Saint Louis but, since a suite with an adjoining

193

bedroom for Elsas and Antoinette was not available, Malissa insisted that Henry pick up the children from the convent that first day and bring them back to stay in the shotgun double he and Malissa owned. Neighbors had kept the house spotless so Malissa had simply hung up the few clothes she and Henry now possessed, and they were, as Malissa put it, "Thank God, home again!"

Henry grinned from ear to ear as he pulled the carriage to a stop in the street. The two children flew into their mother's arms. Dommie knelt on the banquette to embrace them, tears of happiness flowing. Malissa and I bawled, Henry wiped his eyes on his sleeve, the neighbors sniffed and shuffled their feet, dogs barked, strangers stared and the horses stamped nervously at all the wailing. It was a wonderful reunion.

When Henry brought the children from school the next afternoon, I stood in the parlor doorway watching as Dommie embraced all that she could reach. She tried to listen to both of them at the same time, each one vying for her attention. She smiled, touching tenderly and I could clearly see the resemblance: three dark heads, bright, expressive green eyes, the same slender face. Dommie looked up at me with such happiness that I had to swallow hard. I smiled at her, holding fast to the smile as another emotion surfaced. Jealousy? Surely not! Could I be jealous of Dommie's children?

Malissa entered, her face beaming. "Come, babies, see what Aunt Lissa has for you!" Both children turned from Dommie and raced into Malissa's arms.

"Well, I think I've been shown my place!" But Dommie was smiling as she watched Malissa lead the

194

children toward the back of the house. Her smile deepened as she walked to me. "You needn't be jealous," she said softly, "I love Elsas and Antoinette and I love you but it's a different kind of love that I have for them. I want them to be safe and well and I'd die to keep them that way but I also want them to grow up and have a life of their own." Dommie's arms went around my neck, her face close to mine. "The life of my own that I want is with you." We kissed, then, standing in the front parlor of Malissa's cottage. We kissed, our love secure.

* * * * *

The ride back to the hotel was short. As we walked toward the desk I turned my head and saw Blest standing on the other side of the lobby, near the windows that faced Saint Louis Street. I stopped dead in my tracks. "Blest!" I yelled my loudest in that hollow, quiet place, "Blest!" Lifting my skirt, I raced across the carpeted floor and into the thin arms that were outstretched to meet me. "Blest! Oh, Blest!" I hugged her; I lifted her from the floor and swirled around with her in my arms, squeezing her skinny body against mine.

"I thought you were dead, Blest! Oh, honey, I thought you were dead!"

She wiggled out of my arms, her face fiery red. "No, I'm here, I am." Her clear blue eyes looked up at me, "You said you'd take me in, Miss O'Neal. Did you mean it?"

"Of course she meant it, Blest. You're one of the family now." Dommie, smiling, was standing at my side. "And I owe you more than I can ever repay."

Blest was silent for a moment then said, "You're the cousin? You got well?"

"Yes, Blest, I'm the cousin and I got well." Dommie's eyes met mine and her smile widened just the slightest. "Let's go upstairs, shall we? I think lunch and a lot of talking is in order."

* * * * *

We listened, fascinated, as Blest told of her escape through the swamp. She had walked almost every mile of the way to New Orleans-traveling after dark, stealing food, finally buying an old horse with money stolen from Lonnie's chest. I had not noticed the sacks in my excitement but Blest proudly plopped one on the table. I pulled on the dirty drawstring and peered inside. "Blest! There's a fortune here."

"I aim to pay my way, I do." Blest's chin poked out; she was expecting some kind of resistance.

"We don't need your money, Blest, but if the time comes when we do we'll ask for it. Is that acceptable, dear?" Dommie reached to hold Blest's hand.

Blest's grin would have melted the polar ice. "Sure it is, Miss."

"My first name is Dominique, Blest, but those I love call me Dommie. That's the name I'd like for you to use."

I was so glad that Dommie had put Blest at ease. I was happy that they liked each other and proud of Dommie's unconditional acceptance.

"We're all going to look for a house this afternoon," Dommie announced. "One large enough for the three of us and my children. We were told we could buy at auction so we must decide which one

196

will get our bid. We should leave as soon as we've eaten but there'll be plenty of time for talking later."
I looked across the table and met Dommie's eyes. It was a moment of such fullness that I wanted and kiss her.

Dommie spoke again. "Faith was very worried about you, Blest, but you're safe now and we'll all soon have a home . . . together!"

A few of the publications of
THE NAIAD PRESS, INC.
P.O. Box 10543 ● Tallahassee, Florida 32302
Phone (904) 539-5965
Mail orders welcome. Please include 15% postage.

SOUTH OF THE LINE by Catherine Ennis. 216 pp. Civil War
adventure.   ISBN   0-941483-29-0 $8.95

WOMAN PLUS WOMAN by Dolores Klaich. 300 pp. Supurb
Lesbian overview.   ISBN   0-941483-28-2   9.95

SLOW DANCING AT MISS POLLY'S by Sheila Ortiz Taylor.
96 pp. Lesbian Poetry   ISBN   0-941483-30-4   7.95

DOUBLE DAUGHTER by Vicki P. McConnell. 216 pp. A Nyla
Wade Mystery, third in the series.   ISBN   0-941483-26-6   8.95

HEAVY GILT by Delores Klaich. 192 pp. Lesbian detective/
disappearing homophobes/upper class gay society.
                                            ISBN   0-941483-25-8   8.95

THE FINER GRAIN by Denise Ohio. 216 pp. Brilliant young
college lesbian novel.   ISBN   0-941483-11-8   8.95

THE AMAZON TRAIL by Lee Lynch. 216 pp. Life, travel & lore
of famous lesbian author.   ISBN   0-941483-27-4   8.95

HIGH CONTRAST by Jessie Lattimore. 264 pp. Women of the
Crystal Palace.   ISBN   0-941483-17-7   8.95

OCTOBER OBSESSION by Meredith More. Josie's rich, secret
Lesbian life.   ISBN   0-941483-18-5   8.95

LESBIAN CROSSROADS by Ruth Baetz. 276 pp. Contemporary
Lesbian lives.   ISBN   0-941483-21-5   9.95

BEFORE STONEWALL: THE MAKING OF A GAY AND
LESBIAN COMMUNITY by Andrea Weiss & Greta Schiller.
96 pp., 25 illus.   ISBN   0-941483-20-7   7.95

WE WALK THE BACK OF THE TIGER by Patricia A. Murphy.
192 pp. Romantic Lesbian novel/beginning women's movement.
                                            ISBN   0-941483-13-4   8.95

SUNDAY'S CHILD by Joyce Bright. 216 pp. Lesbian athletics, at
last the novel about sports.   ISBN   0-941483-12-6   8.95

OSTEN'S BAY by Zenobia N. Vole. 204 pp. Sizzling adventure
romance set on Bonaire.   ISBN   0-941483-15-0   8.95

LESSONS IN MURDER by Claire McNab. 216 pp. 1st in a stylish
mystery series.   ISBN   0-941483-14-2   8.95

YELLOWTHROAT by Penny Hayes. 240 pp. Margarita, bandit,
kidnaps Julia.   ISBN   0-941483-10-X   8.95

SAPPHISTRY: THE BOOK OF LESBIAN SEXUALITY by
Pat Califia. 3d edition, revised. 208 pp.　　ISBN　0-941483-24-X　8.95

CHERISHED LOVE by Evelyn Kennedy. 192 pp. Erotic
Lesbian love story.　　ISBN　0-941483-08-8　8.95

LAST SEPTEMBER by Helen R. Hull. 208 pp. Six stories & a
glorious novella.　　ISBN　0-941483-09-6　8.95

THE SECRET IN THE BIRD by Camarin Grae. 312 pp. Striking,
psychological suspense novel.　　ISBN　0-941483-05-3　8.95

TO THE LIGHTNING by Catherine Ennis. 208 pp. Romantic
Lesbian 'Robinson Crusoe' adventure.　　ISBN　0-941483-06-1　8.95

THE OTHER SIDE OF VENUS by Shirley Verel. 224 pp.
Luminous, romantic love story.　　ISBN　0-941483-07-X　8.95

DREAMS AND SWORDS by Katherine V. Forrest. 192 pp.
Romantic, erotic, imaginative stories.　　ISBN　0-941483-03-7　8.95

MEMORY BOARD by Jane Rule. 336 pp. Memorable novel
about an aging Lesbian couple.　　ISBN　0-941483-02-9　8.95

THE ALWAYS ANONYMOUS BEAST by Lauren Wright
Douglas. 224 pp. A Caitlin Reese mystery. First in a series.
　　ISBN　0-941483-04-5　8.95

SEARCHING FOR SPRING by Patricia A. Murphy. 224 pp.
Novel about the recovery of love.　　ISBN　0-941483-00-2　8.95

DUSTY'S QUEEN OF HEARTS DINER by Lee Lynch. 240 pp.
Romantic blue-collar novel.　　ISBN　0-941483-01-0　8.95

PARENTS MATTER by Ann Muller. 240 pp. Parents'
relationships with Lesbian daughters and gay sons.
　　ISBN　0-930044-91-6　9.95

THE PEARLS by Shelley Smith. 176 pp. Passion and fun in
the Caribbean sun.　　ISBN　0-930044-93-2　7.95

MAGDALENA by Sarah Aldridge. 352 pp. Epic Lesbian novel
set on three continents.　　ISBN　0-930044-99-1　8.95

THE BLACK AND WHITE OF IT by Ann Allen Shockley.
144 pp. Short stories.　　ISBN　0-930044-96-7　7.95

SAY JESUS AND COME TO ME by Ann Allen Shockley. 288
pp. Contemporary romance.　　ISBN　0-930044-98-3　8.95

LOVING HER by Ann Allen Shockley. 192 pp. Romantic love
story.　　ISBN　0-930044-97-5　7.95

MURDER AT THE NIGHTWOOD BAR by Katherine V.
Forrest. 240 pp. A Kate Delafield mystery. Second in a series.
　　ISBN　0-930044-92-4　8.95

ZOE'S BOOK by Gail Pass. 224 pp. Passionate, obsessive love
story.　　ISBN　0-930044-95-9　7.95

WINGED DANCER by Camarin Grae. 228 pp. Erotic Lesbian
adventure story.   ISBN   0-930044-88-6   8.95

PAZ by Camarin Grae. 336 pp. Romantic Lesbian adventurer
with the power to change the world.   ISBN   0-930044-89-4   8.95

SOUL SNATCHER by Camarin Grae. 224 pp. A puzzle, an
adventure, a mystery — Lesbian romance.   ISBN   0-930044-90-8   8.95

THE LOVE OF GOOD WOMEN by Isabel Miller. 224 pp.
Long-awaited new novel by the author of the beloved Patience
and Sarah.   ISBN   0-930044-81-9   8.95

THE HOUSE AT PELHAM FALLS by Brenda Weathers. 240
pp. Suspenseful Lesbian ghost story.   ISBN   0-930044-79-7   7.95

HOME IN YOUR HANDS by Lee Lynch. 240 pp. More stories
from the author of Old Dyke Tales.   ISBN   0-930044-80-0   7.95

EACH HAND A MAP by Anita Skeen. 112 pp. Real-life poems
that touch us all.   ISBN   0-930044-82-7   6.95

SURPLUS by Sylvia Stevenson. 342 pp. A classic early Lesbian
novel.   ISBN   0-930044-78-9   7.95

PEMBROKE PARK by Michelle Martin. 256 pp. Derring-do
and daring romance in Regency England.   ISBN   0-930044-77-0   7.95

THE LONG TRAIL by Penny Hayes. 248 pp. Vivid adventures
of two women in love in the old west.   ISBN   0-930044-76-2   8.95

HORIZON OF THE HEART by Shelley Smith. 192 pp. Hot
romance in summertime New England.   ISBN   0-930044-75-4   7.95

AN EMERGENCE OF GREEN by Katherine V. Forrest. 288
pp. Powerful novel of sexual discovery.   ISBN   0-930044-69-X   8.95

THE LESBIAN PERIODICALS INDEX edited by Claire
Potter. 432 pp. Author & subject index.   ISBN   0-930044-74-6   29.95

DESERT OF THE HEART by Jane Rule. 224 pp. A classic;
basis for the movie Desert Hearts.   ISBN   0-930044-73-8   7.95

SPRING FORWARD/FALL BACK by Sheila Ortiz Taylor.
288 pp. Literary novel of timeless love.   ISBN   0-930044-70-3   7.95

FOR KEEPS by Elisabeth Nonas. 144 pp. Contemporary novel
about losing and finding love.   ISBN   0-930044-71-1   7.95

TORCHLIGHT TO VALHALLA by Gale Wilhelm. 128 pp.
Classic novel by a great Lesbian writer.   ISBN   0-930044-68-1   7.95

LESBIAN NUNS: BREAKING SILENCE edited by Rosemary
Curb and Nancy Manahan. 432 pp. Unprecedented autobiographies
of religious life.   ISBN   0-930044-62-2   9.95

THE SWASHBUCKLER by Lee Lynch. 288 pp. Colorful novel
set in Greenwich Village in the sixties.   ISBN   0-930044-66-5   8.95

MISFORTUNE'S FRIEND by Sarah Aldridge. 320 pp. Histori-
cal Lesbian novel set on two continents.   ISBN   0-930044-67-3   7.95

A STUDIO OF ONE'S OWN by Ann Stokes. Edited by
Dolores Klaich. 128 pp. Autobiography.   ISBN 0-930044-64-9   7.95

SEX VARIANT WOMEN IN LITERATURE by Jeannette
Howard Foster. 448 pp. Literary history.   ISBN 0-930044-65-7   8.95

A HOT-EYED MODERATE by Jane Rule. 252 pp. Hard-hitting
essays on gay life; writing; art.   ISBN 0-930044-57-6   7.95

INLAND PASSAGE AND OTHER STORIES by Jane Rule.
288 pp. Wide-ranging new collection.   ISBN 0-930044-56-8   7.95

WE TOO ARE DRIFTING by Gale Wilhelm. 128 pp. Timeless
Lesbian novel, a masterpiece.   ISBN 0-930044-61-4   6.95

AMATEUR CITY by Katherine V. Forrest. 224 pp. A Kate
Delafield mystery. First in a series.   ISBN 0-930044-55-X   7.95

THE SOPHIE HOROWITZ STORY by Sarah Schulman. 176
pp. Engaging novel of madcap intrigue.   ISBN 0-930044-54-1   7.95

THE BURNTON WIDOWS by Vickie P. McConnell. 272 pp. A
Nyla Wade mystery, second in the series.   ISBN 0-930044-52-5   7.95

OLD DYKE TALES by Lee Lynch. 224 pp. Extraordinary
stories of our diverse Lesbian lives.   ISBN 0-930044-51-7   8.95

DAUGHTERS OF A CORAL DAWN by Katherine V. Forrest.
240 pp. Novel set in a Lesbian new world.   ISBN 0-930044-50-9   7.95

THE PRICE OF SALT by Claire Morgan. 288 pp. A milestone
novel, a beloved classic.   ISBN 0-930044-49-5   8.95

AGAINST THE SEASON by Jane Rule. 224 pp. Luminous,
complex novel of interrelationships.   ISBN 0-930044-48-7   8.95

LOVERS IN THE PRESENT AFTERNOON by Kathleen
Fleming. 288 pp. A novel about recovery and growth.
                                        ISBN 0-930044-46-0   8.95

TOOTHPICK HOUSE by Lee Lynch. 264 pp. Love between
two Lesbians of different classes.   ISBN 0-930044-45-2   7.95

MADAME AURORA by Sarah Aldridge. 256 pp. Historical
novel featuring a charismatic "seer."   ISBN 0-930044-44-4   7.95

CURIOUS WINE by Katherine V. Forrest. 176 pp. Passionate
Lesbian love story, a best-seller.   ISBN 0-930044-43-6   8.95

BLACK LESBIAN IN WHITE AMERICA by Anita Cornwell.
141 pp. Stories, essays, autobiography.   ISBN 0-930044-41-X   7.50

CONTRACT WITH THE WORLD by Jane Rule. 340 pp.
Powerful, panoramic novel of gay life.   ISBN 0-930044-28-2   7.95

YANTRAS OF WOMANLOVE by Tee A. Corinne. 64 pp.
Photos by noted Lesbian photographer.   ISBN 0-930044-30-4   6.95

MRS. PORTER'S LETTER by Vicki P. McConnell. 224 pp.
The first Nyla Wade mystery.   ISBN 0-930044-29-0   7.95

TO THE CLEVELAND STATION by Carol Anne Douglas. 192 pp. Interracial Lesbian love story. ISBN 0-930044-27-4   6.95

THE NESTING PLACE by Sarah Aldridge. 224 pp. A three-woman triangle—love conquers all! ISBN 0-930044-26-6   7.95

THIS IS NOT FOR YOU by Jane Rule. 284 pp. A letter to a beloved is also an intricate novel. ISBN 0-930044-25-8   8.95

FAULTLINE by Sheila Ortiz Taylor. 140 pp. Warm, funny, literate story of a startling family. ISBN 0-930044-24-X   6.95

THE LESBIAN IN LITERATURE by Barbara Grier. 3d ed. Foreword by Maida Tilchen. 240 pp. Comprehensive bibliography. Literary ratings; rare photos. ISBN 0-930044-23-1   7.95

ANNA'S COUNTRY by Elizabeth Lang. 208 pp. A woman finds her Lesbian identity. ISBN 0-930044-19-3   6.95

PRISM by Valerie Taylor. 158 pp. A love affair between two women in their sixties. ISBN 0-930044-18-5   6.95

BLACK LESBIANS: AN ANNOTATED BIBLIOGRAPHY compiled by J. R. Roberts. Foreword by Barbara Smith. 112 pp. Award-winning bibliography. ISBN 0-930044-21-5   5.95

THE MARQUISE AND THE NOVICE by Victoria Ramstetter. 108 pp. A Lesbian Gothic novel. ISBN 0-930044-16-9   4.95

OUTLANDER by Jane Rule. 207 pp. Short stories and essays by one of our finest writers. ISBN 0-930044-17-7   8.95

ALL TRUE LOVERS by Sarah Aldridge. 292 pp. Romantic novel set in the 1930s and 1940s. ISBN 0-930044-10-X   7.95

A WOMAN APPEARED TO ME by Renee Vivien. 65 pp. A classic; translated by Jeannette H. Foster. ISBN 0-930044-06-1   5.00

CYTHEREA'S BREATH by Sarah Aldridge. 240 pp. Romantic novel about women's entrance into medicine.
ISBN 0-930044-02-9   6.95

TOTTIE by Sarah Aldridge. 181 pp. Lesbian romance in the turmoil of the sixties. ISBN 0-930044-01-0   6.95

THE LATECOMER by Sarah Aldridge. 107 pp. A delicate love story. ISBN 0-930044-00-2   5.00

ODD GIRL OUT by Ann Bannon. ISBN 0-930044-83-5   5.95

I AM A WOMAN by Ann Bannon. ISBN 0-930044-84-3   5.95

WOMEN IN THE SHADOWS by Ann Bannon.
ISBN 0-930044-85-1   5.95

JOURNEY TO A WOMAN by Ann Bannon.
ISBN 0-930044-86-X   5.95

BEEBO BRINKER by Ann Bannon. ISBN 0-930044-87-8   5.95
Legendary novels written in the fifties and sixties, set in the gay mecca of Greenwich Village.